CHIVALRY AMONG VAMPIRES

Book 2
Elders of the Paper Flower Consortium

WRITTEN BY
ELIZABETH GUIZZETTI

Edited by Joe Dacy
Cover and Interior Illustrations by Elizabeth Guizzetti

This is a work of fiction. Names, characters, businesses, places, events and incidents are products of the author's imagination or used in a fictitious manner. Any resemblance to actual persons, living or dead, or actual events is purely coincidental.

Printed in the United States of America

Paperback ISBN-13: 978-1-950708-09-3
Ebook ISBN-13: 978-1-950708-10-9

This book is dedicated to Su Mon and
her love of history and myth.

A Note from the Author:

"Agata looked to be a woman in her thirties, her long chestnut braids went past her waist. Jakub might be a bit older, but not by much. Looking at the Shakespearean beard and mustache and midback curls, Laurence was glad he wasn't stuck with that much hair for eternity."

--Immortal House

So HERE WE ARE, DEAR READERS WITH ANOTHER subgenre in the universe of the Paper Flower Consortium. I knew by the type of man Jakub was before and after his transformation *Chivalry Among Vampires* would be closer to a vampire adventure. Honestly I'm not even sure that "Vampire Adventure" is even a recognized sub-genre, but that is what this book is.

Jakub's story begins on the roads of Moldavia right after his transformation in *Honor Among Vampires*. Jakub and Agata will travel through Moldavia, the Ottoman Empire, and eventually on to the Empire of France. I researched Romanian vampire myths, the former and current culture, and Roman, Saxon, and Ottoman influences upon the Medieval Period. I also had to do massive amounts of research on King Louis XII and France in 1510-1511. France was changing. Some people were trying to hold on to the old ways, others wanted to move forward. De Charny was a real person and considered both then and now, one of France's greatest knights.

Compared to modern culture, Jakub and Agata's views on marriage are old fashioned at best. So how do I write about a couple whose marriage lasted for five centuries?

The same way I would write about a happy marriage today: one filled with mutual respect, love, and trust. Do they make mistakes? Of course. And the elephant in the room is Jakub would believe he is in charge due to his gender.

However I hoped I showed his views on marriage are nuanced and based on Moldavian marriage and divorce law as well as de Charny's views. For example, Jakub believes that to set his lady aside would be a sin. However, if Agata were to leave him, it would be his fault due to his failure to protect her and any other dishonorable actions he might have taken in life.

I also think we tend to view the past with a microscopic lens, that is, we see what we want to see. It's amazing how many people assume people in the Middle Ages didn't bath and have questioned me on that topic after *Honor Among Vampires.*

The cover illustration has a traditional pattern from Romania and France minus the man on horseback. As the symbols in the last book would be close to Agata's heart, the illustrations here are for Jakub.

I want to thank Joe Dacy, who edited this book. I also want to thank my author buddies: N.D. Fessenden beta-read it. And thanks to my husband, Dennis, who has supported me in all my writing.

I hope you enjoy it!

France 1356

Prologue

IN THE WAR-TORN EMPIRE OF FRANCE, THERE WAS not a château, fortress, house, or hut that did not know the Black Death. The winters were cold and dry; the land was barren and harsh. Crops failed. Bands of mercenaries roamed, bored and unfruitful. By order of the king, peasants were forced to rebuild chateaus for the ones destroyed in the war, which had already lasted nineteen years and would span over ninety more.

At Poitiers, the English beat the French and King Jean II or Jean le Bon, was imprisoned. Starving, shamed peasants, called the Jacquerie, revolted against the nobility, acting in the name of their imprisoned king. While much of the violence was in northern France, there were sporadic terrible murders elsewhere. Hundreds of knights, their ladies, and children were slain in the most gruesome of ways. The nobles' reprisals massacred thousands.

As another cold winter loomed, a mason seethed at a landed knight who rode his horse across their village but did not protect it. Each night, he prayed for vengeance. To other men, he bitterly claimed to care Jean le Bon rotted in an English prison, but his mind replayed the gasping deaths of his mother, followed by his wife. The Black Death had ravaged their bodies. Too poor to find a matron, nurse, or widow with milk, his child died of starvation.

One day, the mason woke to find egg-sized gavocciolos underneath his arms. He smiled and hid his disease. On the first day, he set his affairs in order. The next day, his thighs were covered in black spots. Before the infection took over his lungs, he threw himself into the only clean year-round water source for the château. The fall did not kill him, but as he lay broken and bleeding, he took comfort in murdering the knight, his lady, children, and livestock.

He did not succeed in killing his enemy. The knight never even knew of the man's anger. However, the need for a new well stopped the rebuilding of the château and freed peasants from unpaid work.

As workmen dug holes searching for clean water, something old and ancient stirred under the Earth. It churned the dirt, pursuing sustenance. At first, it found nourishment on the mass graves of broken, decaying, putrid flesh.

However, in time, this creature would need something else.

✻

Moldavia

July 1509

Chapter 1

The VAMPIRE, JAKUB PETRESCU CHRISTIAN, sensed the sun's movement toward the horizon. Only a few nights old, he ached for blood, but it would be another hour before sunset. The covered cart's layers of canvas lined with wool and silk tapestries protected him and his beloved wife from the immolating sun.

He ignored his thirst with dreams of the Empire of France. In his previous life as a cavalry officer of Christendom and vassal to both Stephen the Great and Bogdan, the One-Eyed, he had spent more time in battles than home, but he had never seen France. He remembered the drawings of the chapels in Toulon, Nice, Paris, among others. Of the majestic Gothic castle at Boules. He thought of the praise he had heard from French crusaders and mercenaries for the beloved Louis the Twelfth. Jakub could serve the King of the People.

As a boy, he had read *Livre de chevalerie* by the knight, Geoffroi de Charny with great interest and vigor. Before their journey, he reread the treatise to prepare. Though the great knight was captured and killed in the great Battle of Poitiers in 1356 shortly after the book was released, it explained the ethos of the French fighting class. To be a Brother of the Sword with such great warriors was the highest honor Jakub could imagine.

"Did you hear that?" Agata Artuescue Vidraru whispered beside him.

It was strange to experience the road caring for his wife — or any respectable woman. De Charny advised knights to live an austere life and seek basic Spartan accommodation rather than sleep in a soft bed, however as a knight also must care for his lady, Jakub ensured the cart had some comforts for her.

He rolled over and looked her in the face. By the pronounced look of exhaustion, she had not slept again.

"I only hear Castor and Pollux, my love," he said, speaking of the horses, who were outside grazing.

"I am glad you are awake. I feel ... unsafe," she said.

He might only be a few nights old compared to her months of existence as a vampire, but he had familiarity with the road. She never criticized their newly-purchased wagon, but greener than the youngest squire, his poor wife had little experience on which to draw during this adventure. Agata's first sixteen years were spent in her father's town. After they married, she spent the next sixteen raising their five children, running the manor, her dairy, and performing midwifery. Jakub had believed his wife and family were safe in their thickly walled city. He had been wrong.

A dark, furious place in his mind whispered: *I fought for both God and princes. Yet, God allowed a vampire to rape my wife. His own representative murdered her. The nobility dared say I ought to set her aside.*

Away from me, Satan. I shall not dwell in these thoughts. We are leaving Moldavia so we may have a new existence.

In truth, they couldn't stay. Peasant stories claimed vampires were evil and must be rooted out. However, as an important and beloved lady, their town had overlooked Agata's state as long as she remained quarantined, with their eldest bringing her weekly rabbits. She had only killed the man who killed her. No one else. Once Jakub returned home and decided to join her in death, they had to depart.

"Touch your earth, my love, and let it comfort you." He pushed the soft black locks away from her shoulders and kissed her bare neck.

Agata reached for a crock. She rubbed the earth from her garden between her fingers. She took a deep breath.

"Feel better?"

"Yes, my husband. The earth helps me see our children's faces."

The children again. Each dusk their four surviving children were first in her mind, and all five never left her heart.

Jakub thought of Job. *Is it God's will that my wife suffers the loss for eternity, and I suffer her sorrow?* "The children are fine. You gave them a bright future." He kissed her brow. She smiled without opening her eyes. Calmed, she cuddled up to him again, her raven hair spilling across them.

While he rubbed the small of her naked back, he reminded her how their eldest, Irina, was a grown and married woman, pregnant with her first child. She and her husband cared for their youngest, Daciana, who was left a generous dowry. Their two sons had begun their apprenticeships. The townhouse would go to Artur, and money was set aside for Petru to build a house.

He even mentioned Daniella. Out of his and Agata's five children, only Little Daniella did not make it past infancy. They were blessed; not even his elder brother, Count Mihai, had been so fortunate. Mihai's wife suffered two miscarriages, and their firstborn died during infancy before his two sons and daughter came into the world.

"Do you think we might have children in this form?" Agata asked.

"My love, blood taints my seed, and have you had a phase as a vampire?"

She shook her head.

"And the other vampire women you met — had they?"

"I don't believe so. If Phillipa could have children, she would have."

"Then, no, my love."

She snuggled deeper. "That's what I assumed too, but my heart still aches."

She'd lost so much. It pained him he had not been home to defend her.

To protect her now, Jakub followed his beloved wife willingly into undeath. There were unexpected benefits. At thirty-eight, his sword arm had begun to weaken, and his shield arm had an unceasing twinge. His back and shoulders ached. Yet since his transformation, he had not been bothered by any pain. He had a touch of gray in his temples, but Agata's raven hair would always be black as midnight.

"Perhaps, I can relax you," Jakub said.

She nodded and kissed his chest.

His fangs expanded, and he bit down on her flesh. She let him suck gently for a time. It cooled his hunger.

She climbed on top of him. Time slowed as they became one. Time stopped as she bit into his wrist while he was inside her.

✳

Chapter 2

A FTER LOVEMAKING, JAKUB AND AGATA FEASTED upon blood sausage, salted meat, and water until the sky dimmed.

Calmed and satiated, his wife lay back on the tapestry. She closed her eyes and fell asleep. He kissed her on the temple and went to drive the cart.

He unhobbled Pollux and checked the sweet mare's hooves for rocks and other debris before connecting her to the driving shafts. He had just tied his warhorse's lead to the back of the cart and climbed onto the seat when he sensed something terrifying in the twilight. Something as dead as he.

It felt as if a million invisible insects crawled on his skin. He couldn't move. The mass of insects pulsed as one living thing. Their legs crawled, squirmed, writhed upon his flesh, then they burrowed through his eyes and attacked his brain.

A masked figure cloaked in ragged and torn leather emerged on horseback. Jakub had ridden horses his entire life, but he had never seen a horse with long fangs jutting over his thick lips. The gelding's teeth clattered in its muscular jaw in its elongated face. His black tail swished.

The vampire in human form could only be his wife's enemy: Gaius Lepidus Severus, the former Legatus of Carpathia during the Roman empire.

"Agata, run!" Jakub tried to raise his sword, but his

arm couldn't strike against the progenitor of this bloodline. The insects burrowed deeper in his brain. "Agata!"

Agata scurried out of the back of the wagon.

"Remain still." Gaius took the sword out of Jakub's hand. "Remain still."

Jakub couldn't move a muscle. His eyes began to dry as he could no longer blink. In his chest, his heart and lungs began to ache.

"There's no need to fear me, my son. You will be my new Lictor. Stillness."

Even in rags of a bygone era, Gaius moved with the strength and purpose of a wolf. The lush long black hair had a rippling quality and moved as if it had a life of its own. The aquiline nose had once been broken but still balanced his prominent cheekbones and basalt chin covered in a short thick black beard. Like Jakub, he was dead but alive.

Gaius had created the vampire, Nicheloa, who, in the act of deranged cravings, raped Agata, drank her blood, and accidentally turned her into a vampire. Agata had bested Gaius in a battle of wits, and, in vengeance, she asked for Nicheloa's head as her prize. Gaius refused her. Unfortunately for Gaius, he had been a cruel master, unkind to his human servants and vampire women. They had risen against him. He had lost his home, his station, his women.

A man with nothing was always a dangerous foe.

Pollux reared up as Gaius bit into her throat. She had been such a happy pony who enjoyed pulling the cart. Jakub felt sad to see the pony bleed into Gaius's mouth. She stumbled under the vampire's grip. The thirst took hold of him as he watched blood trickle onto the ground. He ached for that trickle.

Castor, tethered to the back of the cart, reared as Gaius moved closer to him. His white socked hooves pattered the ground in panic.

Jakub's heart cried.

Castor was born for war and trained by Jakub's hand since he had been a foal. He had formidable muscles, able to easily spin past pikes, stop quickly, or sprint forward. The horse's strong profile, wide jaw, and deep brown eyes filled with terror in remembrance that horses were prey animals.

Jakub had been silent, because his mouth could make no sound, but as if Jakub had screamed, Gaius looked at him with a strange expression. He grimaced and let the warhorse be.

For a single moment, Jakub felt relief. Then Gaius turned toward him. Terror filled his heart as Gaius opened his linen cămaşa and sliced open his chest. The ancient vampire drank in his life essence until Jakub saw only darkness.

＊

WET BRANCHES TORE AT AGATA'S SKIRTS AS roots grabbed at her legs as she dashed into the forest. Behind her, she heard a gurgle and the unmistakable sound of chains.

Twigs snapped with every footfall. She ducked down; she didn't know which direction to go.

She might run into the horrid forest, or she might follow the road. But where would she go? No one would give her sanctuary. Villagers would kill a vampire.

Another shriek echoed through the wood.

She heard hoofbeats and ducked down behind a tree. A chill started at the base of her spine and worked through to her shoulders. Knees trembling, she clung to the pine, the moss on its bark drenched her shirt front.

Dear God, was that Castor? Or the dead horse, Nix? She tried to block the screams of terror from her mind. She had brought Jakub to this. *What would Gaius do to him?*

"I have to move," she whispered and rose to her feet. She hurried away from the scream. "Stupid woman, do what Jakub said. Move. You cannot help Jakub if you're dead."

The branches and underbrush grew thicker, reaching out and pulling on her loose hair and skirts. Sweat and bloody tears stung her eyes. She could barely see a few feet ahead of her. Yet, fear hastened her steps.

She glanced behind her and saw the silhouette of Gaius in the distance. She couldn't outrun a mounted man, but she couldn't surrender. She dashed into a grassy clearing and pushed herself on even faster. Pain began in her side. Her knees threatened to give. Sheaths of grass pulled on her skirts; a stick ripped at her flesh. She gasped through her throbbing lungs, unable to breathe.

A calloused, icy hand gripped her shoulder. The Legatus spun her around.

"Jakub," she cried. She threw punches and kicks. She might have been hitting a stone statue for all the good it did.

"Your husband can't save you," Gaius hissed in her face as he lifted her by her neck. He clamped an iron around her neck which was attached to a long silver chain. "I've taken most of his blood."

"Jakub!" She tried to grab the chain and run, but it burnt her bare hands.

As if she was no more than a rag doll, he threw her roughly to the ground.

"Jakub will be my new Lictor, and we shall retake my fort. Those harpies will regret raising a hand to me, as will you," Gaius said. By his tone, Agata could see Gaius believed Jakub would simply obey. Perhaps Jakub had no choice, but obedience, if Gaius dominated his mind.

He remounted Nix and urged his horse on to a gallop.

Agata tried to keep up. She tripped and was dragged along to the road. Dirt filled her mouth. Grit lodged itself between her teeth. Rocks and grasses ripped at her clothing, skin, and hair. Finally, he stopped at a wide crossroads. Her face was scratched; her neck was raw.

He pounded a silver stake into the ground and chained her to it. "The sun will rise, and you, and all the problems you caused me, will be gone."

"Jakub will save me!" Agata sobbed, bloody tears running down her cheeks.

Gaius raised his hand as if to strike her. She ducked.

The blow didn't fall.

That was the strange thing about Gaius. He was an ogre, but he couldn't bear to be.

Perhaps if Agata hadn't loved her husband, she might have accepted him as a protector after her transformation. Then she wondered why she even considered it as she remembered that through the ages, he had murdered hundreds, if not thousands, of his concubines. Still, Phillipa survived. She was nearly as old as Gaius was.

"I warned you. Your great love is your downfall. You might have been one of my women. You might have been Nicheola's woman, but no. You had to have your husband."

"Jakub won't ever follow you!"

"Your man is a soldier first, just as I am a soldier. Not even after two thousand years did Phillipa and her harpies ever learn that. You chose your fate. Though Jakub and I shall burn with you, I'll rejoice and live on.

"Jakub will no doubt mourn, but he will forget you in the centuries to come. Once she is dead, no woman is unforgettable."

*

Chapter 3

"JAKUB!" BLOODY TEARS STREAMED DOWN AGATA'S face.

There was no answer except the night birds screaming somewhere deep in the woods. "Calm yourself," Agata hissed aloud. She had to focus on her situation. The sun would rise. She was in the middle of the road. The chain was not long enough to allow her to find shelter in the nearby bushes. Gaius had seen to that.

She clawed at the collar. She wasn't strong enough to bend the metal. She touched the silver chain; it burned her hands. Too soon, the sky grew pink and lightened. The sun peeked between the trees. Her protective shadow would soon be gone.

"Jakub!" No answer. "Jakub!" Still no answer. "Castor! Pollux!"

She cried, hoping one of the horses would hear. No sounds came. Her fangs bit her bottom lip.

She grabbed a handful of dirt and spit upon it. There wasn't enough saliva to make mud. She cut open her arm and added a little blood. It was enough to get a thick layer of dirt to stick to her hands. She carefully picked a single link and pulled it. Earth crumbled off her hands, and the silver touched her skin. She tried to readjust, but each time she brushed the silver with her flesh, her skin blistered. The nightbird's song faded as mourning doves began to coo, and songbirds began to twitter.

She yanked and tugged; her blisters popped and regrew. She screamed into the dawn.

A deep neigh sounded.

"Castor," she called with relief.

The black warhorse trotted toward her, the broken tether dragging behind him.

"Castor! Come here, boy!"

Castor neighed and reared up as she reached for him.

"Castor, help! Please come here."

Agata pulled the blanket from his back and, covering her hands, she tugged at the chain as hard as she could. She thought the link started to give.

She gave it a sharp yank. It remained solid.

The horse nudged her out of the way, he bit down on his blanket. At first, she feared the horse would nip her burnt fingers, but he tugged at the chain.

The stake broke free with a snap.

She tried to climb on Castor, but he reared. She hid her fear of the massive hooves as well as she could. Instead, she whistled then said in a sing-song voice as if the horse was just a giant child: "Come along, Castor, let us find Jakub."

Fortunately, the warhorse agreed and allowed her to hold his tether.

She hoped to follow the horse prints, but there were too many. Castor knew the way back to the cart. Pollux lay dead on the grass. She knelt down beside the pony. There was no pulse under her muscular frame.

Castor neighed and nudged the horse. He curled his lips over his teeth and grunted.

Agata tried to plan. She assumed Gaius had told her the truth, and he would take Jakub to the mountain fort. He had no reason to lie to her. She hoped she could catch up to them.

She covered the wagon with boughs and said a quick prayer for it to be there when she returned. She collected her jewelry, which she hid in her clothes. She wrapped herself first in her woolen traveling suman and then in the loose cow-skin coat with the hope the garments were thick enough to protect her.

Agata showed Castor a bag of oats. He neighed again and let her close to him. She didn't know if she could lift the saddle, so she replaced the blanket on the horse. She tried to mount the horse again. This time he allowed it.

Agata pressed her thighs against Castor's sides, but Castor didn't need her direction and wouldn't have taken it anyway. She leaned forward as the horse galloped down the dirt road and let the horse take her where he was going.

The wind mottled her cheeks and found its way into the coat. She looked to the east as the sun topped the trees. She observed lines of red thread blowing in the wind, caught on trees, in the brush. That had to be a sign from Jakub. The horse's large, flexible nostrils flared. He lifted his head and widened his lips. Then snorted. She wondered if Castor could smell her husband. They were brothers-in-arms after all. They had seen violence together that she could not comprehend.

Her eyes darted along the tree line, searching for another thread. Castor found it first and pawed the ground.

"Calm yourself and think," Agata said. She had no idea how she would beat Gaius. He was stronger; he was ancient. If Gaius died, she wondered what would happen to Phillipa, Sylvia, and Julia. What would happen to Agata and Jakub? They know the agony, she had felt when Nicheloa died. Which meant Gaius and Jakub would have felt it when Agata died. They would not be able to travel. They must have some shelter.

She had beat Gaius once; he still thinks he could outmaneuver her with simple strength. *Maybe Jakub had already beaten him?*

As the sun crested the horizon, Agata found a series

of large boulders that had rolled down the mountains. Some of the spaces between would offer shelter from the sun. She observed a north-facing cave on a cliff face, a red thread was caught between the rocks. Castor curled his thick lips over his teeth and pawed the gravel.

Knowing Castor couldn't climb such a steep, rocky incline, she patted him and left the horse to graze on the side of the road. She gently stepped on the rocks, trying not to make sound and scrambled to the rock shelter.

She peeked into the darkness.

Gaius slept heavily. Nix slept deeper in the cave. In his gloved hand was another chain and at the end of the chain, Jakub slept.

His pallor looked terrible for a vampire. His bare arm was covered in scratches and bruises. Agata had seen this before. Gaius was keeping him weak as he had done to his youngest concubine, Julia.

Agata wanted to hurt Gaius further, but she didn't know what would kill him except the sun or fire. She couldn't chance waking him. Escape was all that mattered.

Silent as most deaths, she crawled toward Jakub and pressed a hand to his shoulder.

His blue eyes fluttered open.

"Take my blood to heal you," she whispered.

Jakub shook his head and pointed at the opening. Holding the chain close to him and slowly wrapping it around his clothed arm, Jakub moved toward Gaius.

*

JAKUB WAS PROUD TO HAVE SUCH A BRAVE AND intelligent wife as Agata but felt self-loathing deep in his chest. *What kind of man, what kind of warrior, am I?* What would his brother, Count Mahai or the other soldiers think of a man who needed his wife to save him?

Holding his breath, Jakub cautiously stepped toward the ancient. Every time a rock shifted under his foot, he feared Gaius would open his eyes. The ancient vampire did not snore, but he did slumber. He slowly unwound the chain from Gaius's glove with each step, taking care that the chain did not clank. Nix's eyes opened and neighed.

Jakub didn't move.

Gaius's fluttered open but closed again. The ancient vampire was either spent or overconfident. Good. Jakub craved killing the vampire who could debilitate them with only a word, he had been dreaming of ways since he had been incapacitated, but first steps first.

He took a step closer. Then another. Waiting to see if those eyes would open, Jakub stretched out his hand and grabbed the keys off Gaius's belt.

Holding his breath, he joined Agata in the shade of a boulder. He glimpsed at their method of escape while shielding his eyes from the sun. "You brought the horses?"

"Pollux is dead, we just have Castor," she whispered.

Careful the silver did not touch his bare skin or Agata's, Jakub undid the chain and collar on his wife. While she rubbed her raw flesh, he unlocked his own.

As soon as he was freed, she murmured, "Come, we must escape."

Gripping her wrist, Jakub hissed in Agata's ear. "We can't just leave him here. He will come after us again. His demon horse moves faster than a cart."

"But we can't kill him. That's why Phillipa, Sylvia, and Julia threw him out. He has strength we don't even know, but I have an idea. We could run the chains across the entrance." Agata whispered.

Jakub didn't know they couldn't kill him. It might only be that the women had not the strength to kill him. "Fear not.

Leave me a gap, but finish your task and stay at the opening of the cave," he ordered.

Agata did not argue.

He returned to the ancient vampire. He unsheathed Gaius's pugio off his belt and plunged the dagger into his chest. Pugios were the weapon rumored to have killed Julius Ceaser and other Roman nobles; it felt right to thrust the leaf-shaped blade deep through Gaius's ribs to the bronze guard.

As the blade went through the ancient heart, Gaius's eyes opened. He shrieked in agony.

Jakub gasped, choked, and coughed.

Nix screamed and bucked.

Agata rounded her body in a quivering, gasping ball among the rocks at the mouth of the cave.

Jakub's flesh moved through a field of razors wounding his skin. He squinted his burning eyes, for a moment, he thought he was blind. No, not blind. Bloody sweat poured down his face.

The undead stallion kicked the walls of the cave, still screaming.

Fearing the worst, Jakub checked his chest. He was unwounded. *I can master the pain.* He pulled the blade from the vampire's wound and let it bleed out.

Jakub pressed his lips to the injury. The blood was ancient, he would have taken his fill and more, but he was in too much pain.

In his moment of triumph, he wanted to filch Gaius's spatha as his trophy, but it was hidden among the Legatus's gear. He needed to care for Agata, and they needed to escape.

"I know it hurts, but we are uninjured." Jakub lifted Agata off the ground and pressed her body to his chest. Her brow slick in a glaze of sweat, and blood stained his shirt.

He covered them both with the cow skin. Careful to remain out of the rising sun, Jakub carried Agata down the steppe. She leaned into his chest to help him keep the weight toward his center. Castor neighed and patted his feet to the ground as they approached.

"Where's my saddle?" he snapped.

Agata cringed and still trembling, whispered, "I couldn't lift the saddle, and I wasn't sure about all the straps, so I left it near the wagon."

He set Agata in the shade of a boulder. "Stay under the skin, my love."

Cursing under his breath about Agata's lack of riding experience and wary of every beam of immolating sunlight, Jakub's knuckles whitened as he adjusted the blanket on Castor.

The sun grew higher.

Jakub pushed Agata on the horse. He climbed up behind her and covered them both in the skin.

Agata whispered, "Don't be angry. I didn't want to hurt Castor."

Jakub patted her leg. "I'm not angry, just worried. If everything you think is true about vampires, Gaius lives, though that blow should've killed him if he were still a man."

"Yes, husband, I still sense him and his pain. And Nix didn't try to follow us or attack. I would think his horse will not leave his side as long as he exists." She explained how she was sure Castor came to get her to save him.

"Which means he may still take his vengeance. We must travel faster. We need to gather what we can and move."

"Yes, my love."

Suddenly she sobbed.

"Why are you weeping?" He wished his voice was more gentle, but he was still trying to master the pain.

She choked out: "I'm sorry for my weakness."

"My wife, you came after Gaius, I could ask for no more," Jakub said. "Cry if you must. Every squire cries after their first battle or when they realize all the stories about great battles are lies. God put us together, only God may separate us," he said with ferocity. "Not a vampire."

He might not have made a killing blow, but he felt virile, comforting his beloved and holding her to his chest.

Jakub was happy to see their wagon had not been vandalized even though they now had no way to move it. (Any good horsemen will tell you a warhorse does not pull a cart.)

After hobbling Castor in a nearby meadow to graze, the vampires ripped into sweet Pollux's decaying horseflesh. They sucked on the coagulated blood and ate her heart, lungs, and kidneys until they were satiated.

Jakub gently dabbed a salve upon Agata's palms and wrapped them to allow the silver burns to heal.

Strong with blood, Jakub tried to pull the wagon. It moved. Agata came up beside him to assist.

"My sweet lady, get on the wagon and call out directions and any obstacles in my way. Fear not, we still have time to cross the mountains and foot lands before the winter snows. But I need more blood to keep our pace."

Over the dirt road, Jakub pulled the cart. He did not genuinely fear to tax his muscles. They would find another cart horse, ox, or sell some of their belongings in the next town. Perhaps they would find a lone traveler to feast upon.

Jakub was simply glad for the action. He didn't understand why he felt so desolate. He remembered himself unraveling the embroidery from his shirt so Agata might follow. And she had followed.

My plan worked, why am I morose? Because I didn't meet a man in battle, I crept up on him unaware.

Does that matter?

It mattered to Jakub, even if it was more important he and his beloved were free.

Every step to the east was a step away from Gaius. The aching desolation in Jakub's heart grew more intense.

Gaius was the only individual who could teach him how to be a vampire soldier.

Certainly, Agata could not. As a human, she was six years younger than he; as a vampire, she was only months older. As educated as she was in the maintenance of a manor and a herd and even womanly arts of healing, she was still a noble woman with no knowledge of war.

*

The Ottoman Empire

October 1509

Chapter 4

THEY HAD MADE IT. DEEP IN THE NIGHT, THEY crossed into the border of the Ottoman Empire with Jakub pulling the wagon. They crossed without seeing Gaius and before the first frost. Yet Agata couldn't stop thinking he might be behind any tree, any building. If he hated her enough to come after her once, he might come again.

She reminded herself that Gaius only found them after she had transformed Jakub. She reminded herself she had lived alone in their manor for months, learning what she could about her condition. She had created two copies of a journal — one for herself and one for their eldest daughter Irina — of everything she had learned about the strengths and weaknesses of vampires. Gaius did not know which village her children lived, but if a vampire ever came for her children, Irina would be ready. And Irina would teach the other children who would pass the knowledge to their children.

I shall use my time on the ships to learn more and send the information to them.

The border guard stopped the cart. He asked why Jakub was pulling the cart.

As planned, her husband answered in Arabic: "Horse limping a bit, that's also why we travel at night."

She heard and understood the word: *Masihiun.* (Christian.) And later the word: "Chilia." Which was the port where they were heading.

One of guards opened the flap to the cart. He didn't seem surprised she was inside. He ran his hands over the tapestries, counting them, but did not speak to her. He spoke more Arabic to Jakub.

Jakub told Agata: "Twenty *akche*."

Agata counted out the 20 silver coins for the duty. She handed it to her husband who handed it to the guard. The other guard scribbled out a receipt and tied a tag to the side of the cart.

They moved on.

They traveled into the night and throughout most of the next day. Jakub only stopping at midday to rest for a few hours.

The sun had set, leaving the sky slashed with gold when Jakub pulled the cart into Chilia. Ahead on smooth dirt streets, the candle lighters ignited oil lamps.

Agata had never seen so many people in one place. The mass of humanity beat with one giant pulse which rang in her ears and made her mouth salivate. They moved past the dockyards, warehouses, and customs houses. With every turn, more humans, cows, goats, and sheep. Dogs and cats skulked around the outside of buildings. Carts and stalls sold all types of cuisines. The spices of the Turks, Greeks, Arabians, Italians, and other cultures fill the air. She had thought that the town she had married into was large, but it was a village compared to Chilia.

As they walked, Agata tightened her grip on Jakub's arm. Jakub adjusted her, so she did not interfere with him, leading Castor.

"What is wrong?" he asked her, his voice gentle.

"I've never seen so many people," she said. "Are all large cities like this?"

"Yes, Wife. I see nothing to fear here. Except us."

He had already told her in accordance with the law, Christians were not allowed to ride on horseback. He had also explained that in the Ottoman Empire, Christian women, especially with northern coloring, were valuable as slaves as were the black girls from Ethiopia and Nigeria. She did not have northern coloring, but her vampiric skin was fair.

"So many different peoples," she said. "Their clothing tells their country."

Around her, most women wore a loose, dark, modestly cut robe that buttoned all the way to the throat over their brightly colored salvar and robes. Their hair and face were covered with a pair of veils. Younger women, perhaps unmarried or the enslaved, wore shorter yelek over their layers of robes. The Ottoman men wore salvar and inner robes covered by longer yelek with decorative seams. On their heads, they wore woolen conical horasani and decorative turbans.

However, the clothing was as varied as the multitude of cultures that spanned the streets. Some women wore embroidered le and fotã under thin shawls like Agata. Their hair covered by maramă if they were married or left free if not.

Men freely donned the iţari, cămaşa, and pieptar with fur căciulă on their heads similar to the style Jakub wore.

She saw short dalmatica-style tunics on both men and women. The impoverished wore browns and yellows, while wealthier individuals wore brightly dyed long garments. A group of simply-dressed, thick-robed Christian monks and nuns crossed their path.

"Look, a Frank," Jakub said.

She saw the man Jakub mentioned. He wore hose under linen breeches. His linen shirt poked out from a bright, short tunic edged in fur. Beside him, a woman wore a long tunic under a long coat, closed in the front with multiple brooches and a belt. Her hair was braided and covered in a linen headdress of the same fabric as the man's tunic.

"What a strange way of dress," she said, referring to the man's hose and codpiece, which exposed the man's lower half so much, he might have been wearing nothing below his tunic.

They crossed an open market, which was now emptying under the fading twilight.

Jakub found the business he sought. "Stay with Castor," he said, though he hadn't needed to remind her.

Agata's gems were already on her person. Her clothing, the manuscript which she wrote upon, and her quills and inks and medical kit were in Castor's saddlebags. Jakub's clothing was packed in a heavy woven sack. Castor's riding saddle was on him but hidden by another blanket.

Jakub went inside. A man donned in salvar and an embroidered kaftcan, which showed the skill of the Ottoman weavers, came out and looked over the cart. He touched one of her tapestries and counted them. There was a bit of bickering back and forth. Jakub went inside with the man again. Jakub returned with a bag of gold. They picked up their personal belongings and led Castor away.

"All these people makes me yearn for blood," Agata whispered. Her lips felt cracked and dry.

"As do I," Jakub said. "But soon, my love."

✳

BRIGHT FLAGS FLEW IN THE BREEZE, AND JAKUB could smell both the Danube and the Black Sea in the movement of the air. Though twilight had faded into the deep of night, many people were still on the streets. He wanted to get out of the Ottoman Empire, following the Muslim dhimmi system, Christians were a protected people with limited freedoms of worship. He kept his weapons packed safely away so no one might see he was armed. Castor was disguised as well as a charger could be as a pack animal. By the look in his eyes, Castor was not pleased.

France also had several sumptuary laws, but as a Catholic and a nobleman, he had better prospects there.

They had escaped Moldavia, and once they hired a ship, the Ottoman Empire. They would sail to Greece, around the Italian Peninsula and on to France.

The French Empire — a land of music and art — had been at war with the English and had seen many losses. It was a land with a great king who needed warriors.

They had already sold the wagon, and not only did they not get what they paid for it, no doubt they did not get what it was worth to the buyer. However, they had limited time at twilight in which to do business.

He wondered how Agata would feel trying to navigate the city during the day. In the thick kaftkans and veils, they might not be seen and protected from the sun. But dressed as Ottomans, someone might think they were spies.

Unlike the scent of animals, the aroma of humans stoked Jakub's hunger. Black, brown, ruddy, tan, white bodies hidden in rich embroidery or humble rags. Humans moved about as if they were fish in the sea, moving about the froth. Not knowing or not wanting to know that two hungry sharks had come into their midst.

He and Agata were still young vampires, but he knew one night he would be ancient as Gaius was ancient. As old as the great serpents of the deep.

She pointed at a painted tower with the base form in a star, is that the church that Stephen the Great and Holy built?"

"Yes, my wife, it is."

Stephen the Great and Holy was a merciless and great commander of men. He had won many wars; however, he had also lost Chilia to the Ottoman Empire. At the end of his life, Chilia remained in the hands of the Ottomans. His son, Bogdan, had other wars to fight.

The stable boy led Castor to a clean stall, and Jakub paid him for Castor's care. He noticed how Agata's eyes counted the money which Jakub paid, but she did not speak. Their adventure was funded by her quickly dwindling treasures. But what were a few gifted tapestries when they had in mortality to gain more? She still had her jewels.

"Let us find a quiet inn for which to do our work," he said.

They moved past several noisy pubs until they found a respectable looking inn. Inside there were plenty of foreign merchants. They would blend in just fine until they could find a ship that would take them to safety.

*

Chapter 5

After securing Agata a private room, Jakub moved through the city until he came to a counting-house. He spoke to a group of merchants about selling more of her treasures to raise the money for passage. Assuming a powerful man like Gaius, or perhaps even his women, might have spies, he told them that he wanted passage to Constanța. Once deals were made, Jakub sought another type of wealth.

The man at a nearby inn had a touch of Hercules in his stance. His thick black waves hung to the middle of his back. His eyes radiated energy and a joyous nature that only the young — or men who have never seen a battlefield — still know. Jakub typically didn't want men, but he wanted his robust and regular heartbeat. And Agata would want him. She would welcome him into her room. Jealousy washed over Jakub.

Was this what it was to face eternity with a wife?

He watched the man. Was this man into men or women? Was he or Agata the better bait?

The man whispered something to a serving woman. The woman scurried away with a smile that told Jakub she was being polite but hoped the man would forget the advance.

Jakub approached. "Do you seek company tonight? My wife and I have traveled long and are lonely for companionship." He rose his eyes to the ceiling and gestured to upstairs.

"Your wife?"

"Is a passionate woman and needs more than any one man can give her."

"You spoil her. The good book says a man ought to beat his wife, so she knows who is the lord and master."

Jakub knew that wasn't true. Unlike this rich, ignorant wantwit, Jakub had actually read the Bible. Still, the man's words held a truth Jakub did not like. By law and tradition, a man had the power to break his wife's spirit. Her happiness was linked to his actions. Agata was made in the image of God as he was. He must treat her thusly.

However, since Jakub planned on killing the man anyway, he said, "She knows I am her lord. But you are not; if she cries out in anything other than pleasure, I'll be doing the same to you."

"I like to ... " The man made a lewd gesture.

Jakub had many experiences when he was at war, but he doubted Agata would have any idea what the gesture meant. He didn't want her to know. He would kill him quickly, before the man suggested such a thing to her.

The candlelight flickered as Jakub brought the man into the private room. Agata rose to pour the wine. Her black hair spilled freely down her back, her luminous skin had a haunting quality, but the man didn't sense the danger. He looked enthralled with her.

His long dark hair spilled toward her as he bowed gallantly.

Holding a cup before their guest, Agata smiled. He stepped closer.

Agata handed him the cup and kissed the side of his neck.

His manhood rose, he didn't seem to notice that her fangs had expanded. In a quick movement, she clamped down on his neck.

"What in hell?" he shouted.

She tore the flesh as he pushed her away. He clutched the side of his neck.

Through the haze of both yearning and repugnance, Jakub stared at the blood spilling from the man's throat. His stomach growled loudly.

Faster and stronger than a human woman, Agata pushed the man against the wall. The sweet-salty smell filled the room, overtaking the stench of the fish and food and pipeweed and the other scents of the city.

The man fell to the floor; Jakub was upon him. He listened to the heartbeat growing fainter. In his mind, Jakub could only see the torrent of blood that this man's veins held.

"You chose well, my love," Agata said, her smiling lips coated with wet, gleaming crimson.

She bent over the man again to have her fill with the man's blood before it cooled.

The blood made Jakub feel alive. Human blood was better than sheep or horse blood; only Gaius had tasted sweeter.

Jakub licked the wound on his wrist, not willing to waste a drop. He swallowed the man's vital fluid like wine until Jakub felt free of the damnable craving. This man who was alive was now dead. He no longer required to eat. He desired to eat.

Jakub sucked the marrow from his right femur and Agata his left.

With his knife, he cut out the man's heart. He plunged his teeth into the bloody muscle. He cut Agata the sweetbreads. They shared the lungs. Chewing on the tough muscle, Jakub delighted in the pleasure of tearing flesh with his fangs.

They ate until they felt fat and sleepy

"We must not be caught with the room in this state," Agata said.

"It is too dangerous to sleep when there's so much

work to be done," Jakub agreed.

Under Agata's direction, Jakub assisted in the carving of the flesh. As he aided her in the horrid work, he wondered if he and Agata were still made in the image of God.

The meat was packed in an oilcloth as if they were any other sailor's rations and tucked into a heavy wooden trunk between layers of salt and kelp to help it keep for the journey. Agata wiped the floor with a rag mop made from the chemise she had been wearing and cleaned the room in the nude.

In the dead of night, Jakub took the man's bones and the rag mop to the harbor. The rag mop was thrown on a trash heap.

"Perhaps, we are devils now," Jakub muttered to himself as he watched waves break on the shore. With a great splash, he dove into the water. His compassion for humans slipped to the bottom of the quay with the bones. He swam until his vampire eyes could no longer see traces of blood on his shirt.

∗

Chapter 6

JAKUB OBSERVED THE ONE-MASTED TRADE-COG.
The overlapping clinker planking, which he could see above the waterline, looked solidly built enough, but the keelplank, was only slightly thicker than the adjacent gardboards. It looked like it might snap in the first storm.

It was an older design, and the open hulled ship hardly seemed the place for Agata, who allowed a sailor to carry her aboard and set her under the canvas tent with their trunks for protection from the sun.

Jakub followed with Castor — who had some sailing experience — though he didn't like it.

Inside, tarred moss clung to the carved grooves and wooden lathes, but tiny beams of light made their way through the hull. It did not give him anymore confidence about the ship.

Jakub brought over Castor's oats, brushed him, and spoke to him in sweet words.

At that moment, he remembered his old master, a great warrior who had taught Jakub in the same gentleness that he taught his hunting hounds and horses. He used to speak to the hunting hounds and his horses as he would any man. He always had time for Jakub's questions and encouraged learning.

He doubted if Gaius had such patience, but he did have answers. Jakub felt lost as the sea lapped against the side of the boat.

"What are you thinking, my love?" Agata asked.

"Gaius."

"I don't believe he is dead; I sense him now and again."

"Then we are well to be away from these shores." Jakub wished he felt relief he indicated to Agata.

The men rowed the cog out of the harbor and then lifted the square-shaped sail.

The sailors' movements created sweat, which pervaded their clothing and the deck of the ship. He thought about taking one, just one, and drinking him dry. He and Agata would dine on his flesh. He must not fall prey to this lust. If he did, he would doom the ship and themselves. They had a trunk of salted flesh. One man died, so the crew could live. One man died, so two vampires could make it to France. Was this what being a vampire was?

To the blazes! I have killed hundreds of men, women, and boys on the battlefield, what is the life of one man? One adulterer? Jakub thought.

As the sun rose, he put on a large floppy hat and slid back deeper beside the crates. Agata had fallen asleep. In the shadows, she snored softly, her hand against the crock filled with earth from her garden.

She had a small smile on her lips. He wondered if she was dreaming of their children. She was and had been a wonderful mother.

There was more Agata had lost. She was used to being a mistress of their home, keeping her herb garden, and herd of cattle. Agata missed his brother's wife, who had been her bosom companion and the other women of their village who she had been friendly due to her work as a midwife and healer. In their town, she was a beloved lady, an important lady. Now Agata was simply Jakub's wife, alone and wandering. Her losses pained him beyond measure.

"My wife is quite ill," he told a sailor.

"Vomit and feel better." The man gestured his hand.

"Already a bucketful, friend. She's sleeping now."

The sailor nodded and went to retrieve licorice root from the captain.

"When she wakes, chew on this," he said.

*

Even THE NIGHT AIR WAS WARM IN CONSTANȚA, but Jakub felt insecure. The salt on his lips taunted his thirst and reminded him of blood. He wanted to move on quickly and get to Greece. Then to the Italian peninsula and on to France. "I feel someone watching," he whispered.

"But Gaius is back in Moldavia," Agata said.

"We ought not to believe he doesn't have his spies," Jakub said. "Or who knows another vampire might be watching. The Ottoman Empire has many great wizards in service to their sultans."

Agata nodded but said nothing. Jakub felt more despondent with each step on the roads of Constanța in which he led Castor. This was the port where the poet Ovid was and spent the last eight years of his life. Ovid wrote the *Trista* and *Epistulae ex Ponto* in which he lamented in the knowledge he would never return home. Jakub was no poet, but he understood the sorrow of knowing he would never return to his beloved Moldavia again.

The journey was so expensive. They would need to kill again in order to make it. Agata was forced to sell the ruby necklace that he had given her on the night of their wedding. Still, she did not speak a word of complaint.

With trunks filled with meat, they embarked on a single-masted, square-sail hulk. There were two castles, one at the bow, one at the stern. A smaller ship than the cog, it had better maneuverability.

The sailors made Agata a comfortable spot under the sterncastle.

Castor neighed uncomfortably, but as he had in journeys past, he made the journey without seasickness.

Agata was not so lucky when it came to seasickness.

Jakub grew used to walking on the moving ship. And he found comfort to the sounds of the water slap the side of the hull. Every morning, an hour before dawn, while the sailors were focused upon their own duties, Jakub did his exercises until the sun rose. In dark linen garments, so the sailors could not see he sweated blood, he practiced uppercuts, lower cuts, and back cuts. He lifted his saddle in the air and placed it down again. He was not sure if death would claim his muscles, but if it tried, he would not let it.

Then, in the shade of the sterncastle, he massaged Castor's legs and brushed him as the sun rose. To pass the time, Agata asked questions in French while Jakub answered questions in the same. They practiced French courtly mannerisms and discussed French fashion.

Sometimes, Agata sang donias to Castor. The stallion seemed to be getting used to her ministrations though he preferred Jakub. He liked to rest his massive head on Jakub's shoulder while he listened to her songs.

Once the seasickness had passed, Agata returned to her studies. She recorded observable changes or the lack of change. She recorded their hunger and strange cravings.

Each night, she prayed to God for their children's safety and future. She wistfully spoke about the grandchild she would never see and wrote letters to Irina.

In Jakub's dour moments, he sometimes thought about how their universe was just this ship and the sailors moving around them. Only when he slept, he indulged in his monstrous cravings and undying thirst. Otherwise, he fantasied but dared not touch the sailors.

To give into his cravings would mean his, Agata, and Castor's death.

*

Chapter 7

THE FIRST CROSSING HAD BEEN REASONABLY smooth, but deep in the Black Sea, the boat swayed to and fro. Agata did not want to complain about the rocking sea, but she was glad for the licorice root, which kept the vomiting at bay. Jakub had fallen asleep, leaning against Castor, who also slept nestled in the hay. But they both had been at sea before.

She peered out above the hull, she saw black waves crested with white and gray mists. She could no longer see the land. Jakub told her such wondrous stories of the land of the Franks. She hoped the Empire of France would be all he believed it would be. But she had no hope for herself.

The boat pitched another way. She cried out and held tight to the railing.

A sailor gestured at her and tried to speak, but it was in Arabic.

She bowed her head and showed him the licorice root.

He gestured to a bucket and moved his feet like he was slipping. She guessed he meant the deck was slippery.

She nodded and gestured sleep.

He nodded back to her.

She returned to the sterncastle with an aching heart. She tried to ignore the lump in her throat. The raindrops which fell on the deck mixed with her tears. She could never go home. The last time she embraced her daughters, the scent of their flesh made her want to bite their throats.

"We made the right choice for the children," Agata whispered to herself.

The children are safe from me. And Gaius. Phillipa is keeping the old truce between the vampires and human villages, she thought to her crock of earth, trying to comfort herself.

When she touched her earth, the voices of her children came to her. Their songs, their donias, their games. She regretted every time she scolded or switched them. She rejoiced in the memories of playing peek-a-boo, teaching them to read and write, or when she kissed their brows if they were troubled.

She thought of Irina's wedding, how she now wore her hair in a married woman's coil, and had a child on the way. Artur, a vassal of Count Mihai, followed in the footsteps of his courageous father. Petru apprenticed under Irina's husband. Daniella buried in the family plot. And little Daciana lived with Irina.

She thought of Jakub's family, especially the wife of his brother, Gavrilla. She missed her friend with an intensity she had not imagined.

Away foul spirit. They are not lost to heaven, they live on. Safe. Perhaps once we are settled in France, I might even correspond with them.

The ship seemed to pitch more furiously as she lay awake thinking about the children, her sister-in-law, and all the babies (human, cow, dog, and the occasional sheep) that she had helped bring in the world. She didn't regret killing her rapist, Nicheloa, or the priest, Bogdan, who murdered her. She realized she didn't even mind killing the young man in Chilia, so Jakub and she might make this journey.

Jakub had tried to keep the man's brutality from her, but she had sensed the man had been an ox. She hadn't exactly known what he wanted, but she knew if he had found a girl without protection, he would have shamed her and abandoned her to the fates. It was right to kill such men.

Holding her cloak tight, she peeked out again. Storm clouds covered the sky, blocking the light.

The crew scrambled to action in a frantic pace as rain poured furiously down upon them. In every direction were swells of hideous gray and white.

Agata heard another cry in Arabic. A sailor ran over with thick bindings and babbled to Jakub, who threw on his coat.

Jakub tried to smile as the sailor tied them to the mast.

She felt flayed by each droplet of water, but her skin grew numb and cold, the spray lost it sting. Her maramă was ripped away in the wind. She clutched at her cloak tighter.

Jakub's eyes looked at her with a coldness as if Agata was a stranger. The thought warped her mind as she stared at her hideous and hungry, undead beloved.

"Do you think we will succeed? Will we make it to France?" Agata asked.

"Why ask such questions? God put us together and only God could tear us apart. Do you fear, perhaps, God controls this storm? There's nothing I can do. I know about horses, not ships." Yet the cold nothingness lifted from his eyes. "I hate being powerless against the sea. Sailors are no more powerful, but ride with Neptune's blessings."

A wave poured over them. Another wave pummeled them from the other direction.

"I would pray to Neptune if I thought it would do any good, but I doubt Neptune's mercy as much as I doubt Jehovah's." He shouted over the sound of the waves.

"Perhaps Salacia!" Agata said in jest. (Neptune's wife, Salacia, is the personification of the calm and sunlit sea.)

Jakub invoked her name, but it did not calm the sea.

Agata choked on seawater. Were they sinking? She couldn't see. Jakub appeared as the boat pitched again. A crack of lightning brightened the sky.

Agata clasped Jakub's closer arm and wept. She vomited on the deck, but another surge splashed the bloody vomit away. "I love you," she said.

"What?" he shouted.

"I love you," Agata shouted over the sound of the waves.

With his free hand, he stroked her wet white cheek until it was over. The wind died. And the sea calmed as if the storm had never been.

Once the sailor undid the binding, Agata collapsed into Jakub's arms. He carried her back to their space under the sterncastle. Castor was soaked and annoyed but survived. So had most of their trunks.

A fish flopped on the deck.

A sailor cut it open and gave the flesh to Agata and gestured for her to eat.

Jakub said, "He said, 'For the little mother's strength.'"

Agata accepted it with a bow of her head. Jakub thanked the sailor in Arabic.

When they were alone, Agata and Jakub sucked the flesh from the spiny bones.

✳

Dear Irina,

I hope this missive finds you well. I pray nightly for the health of you, your husband, your brothers, sister and your newborn infant. Is it a boy or a girl? What name have you christened him?

Though there has been some dangers crossing the mountains, and we rode many ships, we can now see the coast of France. Your noble father is greatly pleased as am I. Castor cannot speak of course, but I am sure the horse longs for solid earth under his hooves as we both do.

Enclosed is two more recipes one which your father and I tried in Moldavia and one which I gathered in the Italian Peninsula.

With all my love,
Mother

On the next page, written carefully in code and disguised as ways to salt fish were descriptions of how to trap a vampire with silver chains.

*

Empire of France

July 1510

Chapter 8

IN A TINY FORGOTTEN VILLAGE, A BOY OF SEVEN called for his family's missing goat. His voice carried in the darkness. He could hear his elder sister in the distance, also calling. The pen had not been left open, but the goat was gone. It was not his fault—or hers. But they feared returning home without the animal.

In his worries, he didn't notice the tentacle writhing along the ground, feeling the tremors of earth. It had found other tasty prey in the area and searched for more. The boy hardly had a chance to scream when it slithered up his leg and grabbed him around the chest. He was fortunate, the thing which squeezed him crushed his bones. He was dead before he was dragged under the earth.

His sister was not so lucky. It grasped her ankle and squeezed. While her bones were crushed, she hit the ground alive. She pressed her eyes shut trying to stop the ripping of her flesh. Earth pressed in on her, smothering. Her mouth and nostrils filled with gravel and dirt, she sputtered. Her lungs ached to breath, but filled with viscous, slimy mud.

*

WITH FIVE LEGS OF THE JOURNEY COMPLETED, the ship sailed from the Mediterranean in between two large stone towers to a bay and the royal port of Toulon. Jakub's heart soared. Brushing his horse, he spoke happily to Castor: "I must fulfill military service, but the French nobility has explicit lawful and financial privileges. We'll have the right to hunt, and my beloved wife will dine on venison each night.

"More importantly, I can wear a sword and ride you instead of leading you."

Castor neighed and nodded as if in agreement. A warhorse should not have to disguise his natural poise. Plus, the horse was no doubt glad to be getting off the ship.

Jakub was pleased with his first glimpse of the Empire of France looked precisely as it had in his dreams.

He held his breath and checked his wide-brimmed hat as the sun peeked out from behind the clouds. Even with his limited view, he saw the white towered manor surrounded by gardens. Behind the towers, mountains rose even higher. Below, a fishing village surrounded by a stone wall with a large chapel reached toward the sky. Gulls cried their haunting songs as they ascended on the funnels of sea-wind and dove into the water.

Under her veils, Agata got on her toes and clasped Jakub's hand.

"You did it. We are in France!" she whispered excitedly. She embraced him around the neck and kissed him. "Look, isn't the chapel beautiful?"

Jakub's attention was on the large manor house, but Agata would want to give thanks to God and pray for the children.

Jakub tried to plan as the ship approached the harbor, but he was not sure how to proceed. He did not want Agata to worry. He had letters of introduction and recommendation written by his brother and Voivode Bogdan III. However, he must connect with the French nobility in order to ensure his success at court.

He quickly wrote two letters: one to the count and on to the mayor of Toulon petitioning for their assistance.

He found the captain and asked if the cabin boy might run an errand for him.

"What errand?"

"Bring this letter to the Count of Provence. I will pay you both a franc for your trouble." As soon as the ship brushed the side of the dock, the boy dashed off.

With Agata wearing layers of veils and Jakub in a wide-brimmed hat, they traversed a labyrinth of docks and buildings. Other than fashions and color of the heraldry, the French port of Toulon was not much different than the Moorish ports. Longshoremen buzzed around the docks unloading and loading ships. Passengers hurriedly embarked ships. Sailors swaggered drunkenly. Families embraced. Beyond, brothels and cardrooms lined the docks.

After the stop at the customs house, where they paid a sizable duty, Jakub observed the old Roman aqueducts were in ruins. He suggested Agata ride Castor and met Castor's eyes. The man and his warhorse had a moment of understanding as they had when Jakub had ridden into battle. Agata was safer if she was astride the horse.

Garbage and human feces lined the streets. Dogs and cats roamed, hunting for scraps.

They passed a series of warehouses and an open market which was still bustling in the twilight. Someone coughed nearby. Jakub scanned the crowd for weakened prey. They would need blood if they were to meet the count. Two men pushed a cart piled high with bags of flour past them. A group of women carried bundles on their heads and children on their backs. Men with sacks slung over the shoulders. Older children played in the shadow of the tower. Wealthy individuals rode horses or rode in carriages in their delicate embroidered fabrics, but what surprised Jakub was the small black patches of silk or velvet in contrast to their full face of ivory cosmetics. One or two were pretty enough, but some faces were sprinkled with them.

They drew near to the church. He helped Agata off the horse, and they went inside the stone building.

The large elaborately carved and painted wooden retable surrounded the alter.

Agata bowed her head as she crossed herself.

Jakub crossed himself out of habit and to please his wife.

When he didn't speak, Agata began: "Father, Son, and Holy Spirit, Holy Trinity of love, we praise you for keeping us safe during our journey and bless you for calling us to be your holy people. Remain in our hearts. Guide us in our love and service. We praise you now and forever. Amen!"

"Amen," Jakub repeated.

Jakub escorted Agata to the candles where she lit a candle for the children.

He gestured at a priest. "My lady seeks communion."

"Just your wife?"

He wasn't sure if he ever believed in God. Not how deeply Agata believed anyway, but he said, "Both of us."

The priest listened to Agata's confession first. They spoke a few minutes in private, and she left the confessional with a downcast look upon her face.

Jakub went into the confessional. He spoke of being short-tempered with his wife for her ignorance. The priest's heart skipped a beat.

Jakub spoke of missing his men and not knowing where God led them.

The priest's eyes never left Jakub's face as he spoke of sin and repentance. His lips glistened as he spoke of Jakub's penalty.

Jakub nodded but stopped listening as he would not wear sackcloth beneath his clothes or fast in prayer. In their former town, the town gate was carved with the words: "God is love."

Jakub wasn't sure if God was love in France, he hoped

it was only this particular God's representative was simply a wantwit. The last priest who thought to come between Agata and the ones she loved wound up dead.

He salivated at the thought of killing the man. His fangs pressed against his gums. Fearing the other people in and near the cathedral, he took his wife's arm and hurried out of the church without violence to the idiot.

"Whatever he said to you, I want you to forget. He was a bumbler who mingled the truth with his own ideas," Jakub said gruffly to her and kissed her hand.

"I am ready to meet the administrator of the county," Agata whispered from behind her veils.

"Before we eat?" Jakub asked.

"After, but I believe its best if we go as soon as possible. We don't want to accidentally insult them," Agata said. "I fear this place. The patches on the faces and other customs seem so strange."

They found a butcher, bought two thick steaks from a cow's loin. Hidden in an alley, they ate them raw.

*

Chapter 9

AGATA WAS CAREFUL NOT TO STEP INTO THE sunbeam as she removed her veils. Jakub appeared to be walking with less care, but she did not speak a word against him. He had a plan, and they must see it through.

Lit candles flickered about the parlor and were reflected in polished mirrors. Agata hoped no one would notice that only their clothing was reflected in the brass, not themselves. The curtains were open. The smell of the sea, humanity, and animals drifted inside, but her nose was tickled by the sweet orange perfume, tallow, and burning paper.

"Welcome to Provence, my foreign friends," Estienne Hamon the Count of Provence said in a deep bass voice which seemed younger the rest of the man.

Jakub bowed and replied a few general kindnesses toward the countess — a woman who looked to be a decade senior to Agata, but a decade younger than her husband. Her hair was covered with a wimple and veil. As was common in French fashion, her conical gown artificially widened her hips while exposing more of the breast than what is modest in Moldavia. *Soon, I must learn to dress in such a way.*

Agata curtsied.

He waddled slightly in his heavy garments, which covered his burly frame. His wide-necked satin blue doublet strained against his stomach as he sat down. Thick strips of alternating colors in red and blue and gold ran up his arms.

His shirt bore a large frill edged in black at the neck and wide ruffles at the wrist. On a heavy golden chain, he wore a gold amulet with a deep blue sapphire to match his doublet.

The Count of Provence might have once been dashing. A Roman nose and high forehead sat above loose jowls. His round brown eyes were lined with heavy lines, but Roman features didn't surprise Agata. Who knew? This man might even share a bond by the blood of the same ancient ancestor to Jakub or Agata.

Jakub had told her this part of the Kingdom of France shared much history with their own Moldavia— which before the Roman occupation in 106 AD was the Kingdom of Dacia. She knew during the 2nd century BC, the people of this area appealed to Rome for help against the Ligures who invaded them from north-western Italy. The Roman legions entered the area now called Provence three times.

Beside her, Jakub's muscles tensed as the count kissed her hand.

The countess claimed to be glad to meet the daughter of a foreign count.

"So, how may I help you, honorable son of Peter?" the count said.

"I have come to join my French brothers-in-arms. There are many wars. Your king is magnanimous. Louis XII is a king of the people, they say."

"He is, but as of late, he is more concerned with the lack of a son. His first queen was sterile. His second queen had several miscarriages, stillborn son, and two daughters," the count sighed. "Many a son has died in the wars ... now it seems more are on the horizon. Ah, well, cest la vie."

"What of the daughter?" Agata asked.

"What of her?" The countess asked.

"Will she inherit?"

"In France, daughters do not inherit the throne. Our majesty will ensure his family's inheritance through betrothal," the count said.

"I hope she will be happy in her marriage." Agata crossed herself to bless the girl she had never met.

"What hope is there for that?" the countess whispered drolly to Agata, but loud enough, the men could hear.

Agata spoke to the countess on marriages, of her children and theirs, and other womanly matters. The countess's children were safe with their nurse, but many other children of France were starving. Through the spoken word and unspoken look, she learned many of France's counties were reeling from unending wars and famine.

*

THE COUNT EXCHANGED A KNOWING LOOK WITH Jakub that said one thing: *Women.* It was apparent the nobles did not have a happy marriage. Nor did the count care. Jakub chuckled, but he was wary of a man who didn't love his wife and children. He was even more suspicious of a man who dressed in luxurious silks and jewels while wearing a slender gold-handled rapier on his belt and a black velvet star over his eye.

The count was not what Jakub expected from the nobility of France. French law required the count to see military service. In *Livre de chevalerie,* de Charny guided knights to be reasonable and measured in their eating, keep their bodies healthy, and avoid luxurious clothing. De Charney would have hated the layers of silk.

Jakub thought of his brother, Count Mihai, who, due to their birth order, never ventured from the safety of their town. He was a competent administer, but he had not, nor ever had been, a warrior. Though Count Estienne wore a sword, perhaps he was not a warrior either, but had a younger brother who served in his stead.

The gem Count Estienne wore danced in the firelight and hypnotized Jakub. He dreamed of tearing out the count's fat throat and drink his blood dry. He would bestow the gem on Agata. He envisaged the gem hanging between Agata's naked breasts. He pushed the thought away.

Agata asked, "Do you enjoy the ongoing of the court?"

"Unfortunately, Blois is too far for my husband to travel," the countess said with marked bitterness.

The count cleared his throat. "Madame, this port has only been part of the Kingdom since 1486 when Provence joined the empire. Have you seen much of Provence?"

"We came directly after we gave thanks in the chapel for our safe journey. We wished to be right with God as well as man," Jakub said.

"Indeed," the count said. "Our chapel is lovely, isn't it? The present building was begun in 1096 by Gilbert, Count of Provence in gratitude for his safe return from the Crusades."

Jakub must have missed something in the count's words or behavior because the count stopped talking. "Perhaps I offended you."

"No. I love history, Count, at times listen quite intently. Forgive me for it," Jakub said. "Perhaps, you might enlighten me of your magnificent community, if it pleases you."

By the glimmer in the count's eye, nothing would please him more. "Oh, how I wish my son was as interested in our history as you, Sir Jakub. Perhaps you, a knight of Moldavia, would be a good example to him.

"Stay tonight, and experience our table."

Jakub learned, even decades later, France's counties tottered from shortages of everything but war. And he learned Count Estienne did not consider Provence part of the French Empire.

✳

Chapter 10

"I NEED TO HUNT NOW," JAKUB WHISPERED, lightheaded with the lack of fresh blood. He only had minimal amounts of cooked animal flesh with vegetables and stewed fruits for several days. The old pains moved through his joints. His neck ached. "If only we could find a lost servant or better yet a brigand."

With the Count of Provence's letter of introduction to King Louis XII, they rode toward a series of wooden and thatched huts. The poor ought to have some sick.

"As do I," Agata replied. "My head aches terribly."

"Have you learned why the count and countess wore those small black velvet patches?" Jakub asked, hoping to distract his wife from her pain.

"To cover mars in their complexion so each one can a beautiful porcelain doll."

"You will do this?"

"I shall do what is necessary, my love, but our skin is pale enough without paint."

Out of the corner of his eye, he saw three forms dressed in rags slink out of a window. They moved too quick to be human.

"Vampires," Agata whispered beside him.

He did not know if they would be friends or foes. They did not wear swords, so they must be commoners.

"Hail, I am Jakub Petrescu, Son of Count Petru. This is my wife, Agata, the daughter of Count Artur."

The largest man did not reply with his name, but said, "We are Jacquerie. She is your lady?"

Jakub didn't feel the slightest fear though he knew who the Jacquerie were. He tasted Agata's distress in the sound of her pulse.

The two men, who had not spoken, lunged at Agata and caught hold of her skirt and yanked her off Castor. Jakub's heart cried at the ghastly expression of wide-eyed horror on his wife's face as she screamed. Her vulnerability and fear of ravishment overwhelmed him.

Agata tried to swing a fist at her assailants, but she didn't have any power in her blows. She collapsed as a punch struck the side of her head.

As Jakub expected, it threw the man who held her weight off balance.

Jakub barreled into him, his second blade drawn.

They tumbled onto the dirt road. The man released Agata as Jakub's knife entered the attacker's chest, crashing against his ribs. Jakub retracted his blade and slashed the man across the throat. Blood bubbled to the surface and splattered against his lips, mesmerizing him. His fangs expanded in want of blood, but as it had on the battlefield, Jakub's mind achieved a strange mental state of calmness. He was aware of each moment of this battle. They were commoners with their hands and cudgels. He had a dagger and a sword.

Agata screamed.

He leaped to his feet. He sized up the next two thugs. So had Castor.

The warhorse got between Agata and the man pursuing her. He kicked him squarely in the chest. The man fell back, but then sprang onto Castor's back.

The final man, the one who spoke, swung his cudgel at Jakub's head. He parried each blow. He struck out when appropriate.

Out of the corner of his eye, Jakub saw Agata haul his shield in the air and dash it against the man who held Castor. The pointed end of his shield entered the attacker's flesh. He fell to the ground.

Castor reared up and pummeled the man on the ground with his iron shoes.

The vampire screamed as Castor's hooves rained down.

Jakub slashed his sword down in front of his foe, forcing him to stop short. And in this hesitation, the next blow decapitated him.

The third vampire had escaped Castor's hooves and tried to jump upon him. Jakub threw him off his back and cracked his skull with his pommel. He wanted him to feel the pain that his sweet wife felt. His sword cut through flesh and bone.

Once the vampires were wailing, incapacitated, he carved the three vampires into pieces. He knew they still lived; still felt the agony from his blade. Somewhere an older vampire felt the loss of his children. He told himself these common vampires were nothing to him, but each time his blade dug into their still living flesh, he felt a strange gladness. If only they had been worthy opponents, rather than commoners, he might have felt joy.

"Drink of them and become strong, my beloved," he said.

Agata knelt down and sucked from the bloody remains. The vampires whose heads were more or less intact opened their mouths in agony. He gorged on the most tender organs. He popped an eye into his mouth and crushed it with his teeth. He bit into the kidneys and devoured their sweetness. He felt stronger than he had in days.

He cut out another set of kidneys for Agata. After they had their fill, Jakub spread out the body parts in a glade.

"We might have been allies, but now you will burn

in the coming day," Jakub said, his mind suddenly went to Gaius. The ancient vampire was laughing.

Jakub found the vampire's trail and followed the vampire's footprints to a low stone grotto. They had to duck to go inside, but the room opened up. Massive boulders lined the gravel floor, which the vampires had used as makeshift tables or bunks. Leather bags and clothing rotted hanging from a line that crossed two natural pillars.

A statue of the Virgin looked down upon them.

Water had carved out the limestone cave. A small creek ran through the bottom. Agata tested it and told Jakub it was fresh. Castor guzzled the clean water. Jakub went out and harvested leaves and grasses.

She built a fire in the fire ring and went through the vampire's belongings. She found a few coins within the rags but little else of value. The cloths fueled their fire.

A cave filled with bugs is no place for Agata. I failed my wife again. He almost wished she would complain and nag at him, but no word of grievance or criticism came from her lips as she moved back toward the opening of the grotto.

He wanted to pull her back deeper inside, but the sky was still dark, and rain had begun to fall.

"What are you doing?" he asked, trying to shake away the feeling of claustrophobia working its way through his humors.

"Watching the raindrops," Agata said slowly. "Would you like to join me?"

"No."

"Once we get settled," she said.

Settled.

"I shall be returning to my former profession."

He didn't answer her. *She once asked for my permission, now she dictates.*

"Do you still love me, Jakub?" Agata asked, breaking the silence.

"You are my wife," he said, with the hope that would be the final word. It wasn't.

"But we are vampires, and eternity is a long time," Agata said.

"We make our own heaven and hell. Apparently, your heaven is looking after pregnant women."

"And building things that grow. Perhaps I'd even like to take in children someday."

Jakub scowled. "Child vampires?"

Perhaps the old stories were true. *Had Agata become like Lamia, destined to destroy all who loved her?* After all, they left Moldavia to ensure their children would be safe. But what of France's children?

"No, my love, orphans who we might raise. Though I fear Gaius finding us if we do, we might make them into vampires as adults if they wish."

"Sounds like hell." Jakub said.

"What is your idea of heaven?" Agata asked so softly her voice was barely audible over the rain.

"Having something to fight for, something to protect."

"Besides me?"

"Something bigger than you. I miss being an officer ... I was a good officer. If you hadn't been attacked ... why were you in that barn? That's what we paid Robert for."

"I ... "

"What's a cow and a calf to our lives? To a herdsman's life. Robert is dead and is at rest. We are dead, but we walk! Perhaps Mihai was right. I should have put you away."

A bloody tear slipped down Agata's cheek, and she clutched at the cross she wore at her neck. "I offered you freedom once. I won't stay with you if I pain you so. I have no need for eternal misery."

The idea of losing Agata terrified him. It wasn't only that he loved his wife. She was the mother of his children. She created their home with thoughtfulness, and until the attack, it had been a place of joy. However, he felt a more profound fear. If she was lost to him, despair and bitterness would defeat his better nature.

"You are my wife. I swore to protect and provide for you. You swore to obey me."

"We swore till death. We have both died. We can make our own rules now. Stay with me in love or leave me."

Her words created an icy spot in Jakub's soul. He felt like a raindrop cascading from the clouds to the earth, not knowing where he would end up. Worse, though he was snapping at her for her foolishness, he thought *I should have been there.*

"And if I leave you to your fate? Then what?"

"I don't know where God will lead us. I suppose I shall find a village and try to midwife again. You can find a war to fight in," Agata said in an unwavering tone. "But it is not my fault that France is not the place you dreamed it to be."

"No, it is not," Jakub admitted.

"You knew what he meant when he called themselves Jacquerie," Agata demanded.

"Jacquerie were peasants who revolted against the nobility over a century ago during the French and English conflicts. They killed knights and their ladies because mercenaries were attacking and raping commoners. The nobility were stuck fighting a war over who was king of France and could not help them."

"If you hadn't killed them ... "

It annoyed Jakub that Agata was asking questions she knew the answer to, but he said, "The vampires planned to kill and rob me, they would have raped and killed you. Evil men are the same as evil men everywhere."

"Then it is good that we ate them," she said matter-of-factly. "I felt guilt, but no longer."

✻

Chapter 11

JAKUB AND AGATA BARELY SPOKE, THOUGH HE felt her sweet breath on the back of his neck as they rode Castor. They traveled at night when most humans, except a patrol or a drunk farmer, were in bed.

The French countryside had regressed to an antediluvian state. Former Roman roads had degenerated to bumpy, potholed, and furrowed dirt paths barely large enough for two carts to pass side by side. Jakub worried about Castor twisting an ankle or throwing a shoe.

"It would be better if Castor had our eyesight," Jakub muttered. "This must be why Gaius changed his horses."

"Undeniably, my love, it might be," Agata said thoughtfully. "But we will need meat and blood for one more and may not be able to stable him if he is a vampire."

What does Agata know of stabling a horse and his care? She had never ridden a horse before she became a vampire. His thoughts were broken by a young buck in a clearing.

"But I'll help you transform him, if ... ," she said quickly as if she suspected she had angered him.

"Shhh. Hold."

He put his hand up and pointed at the buck. He glanced around and drew his crossbow. Knowing they couldn't chance being caught poaching, he carefully aimed. The bolt flew through the air.

The shot penetrated the buck's hide.

The deer took two steps and fell.

Glancing around again, Jakub lifted the carcass to his shoulders and carried it deeper into the forest before he cleaned it.

Agata made a fire.

Once the animal was cleaned, Jakub carved the meat. Agata put a shoulder onto a spit and cooked it over their fire. It smelled heavenly. They hung the skin and rest of the flesh to dry over the smoke.

At first, the sound was no more than a faint murmur, shuffling leaves by the wind, a broken branch. Yet Jakub's senses, honed in battle, detected that undead approached. Noxious rage built inside him as he thought of the vampire who had grabbed Agata.

"Someone's coming," he told her.

He and Agata gulped the deer's blood deeply, quickly to prepare for the vampires.

"I have a sword," he shouted.

Agata dashed toward Castor.

A female wearing ripped green and white fabrics approached first. Behind her, twenty vampires in rags skulked at the edge of the clearing. Perhaps the first had been a lady, but the rest were simple peasants who had the unfortunate experience of being turned into vampires.

"We have no quarrel, but there are more of us, and we are hungry. The winter has been hard," the woman said in French. "If you wish to keep your horse, leave."

Jakub raised his sword.

Laughter and whoops answered them. Sounds of hideous starving mania.

The horde of filthy monsters crept closer. The vampires wanted nothing to do with them. Behind them, more vampires gathered and pushed them away from their bloody prey. Jakub lifted Agata on Castor. As quickly as he dared, Jakub led Castor into the darkness.

Were all vampires in France so low?

*

AGATA COULD SEE THE PINES AND UNDERBRUSH and blackness beyond. Her stomach growled; her lips and tongue felt like sand. She tried to think of the sweet taste of deer blood, but the few sips had not satiated her. She thought of the vampire flesh she had eaten weeks before.

Agata felt the French vampires' presence in every breeze and movement in the underbrush. She feared they would follow. Mile after mile, they slowly moved northwest farther from the pack of hungry vampires who may or may not be their enemy.

Jakub plastered a wane smile on his face, each time he looked back at her. Agata knew that smile was for her benefit. He was worried and hungry too.

Their silk tapestries were gone; only a few of her precious jewels remained. They had bits of gold and silver from their victims, but not enough to buy a place at court. Hopefully, the last of their wealth might buy them an appropriate wardrobe.

They found a farming hamlet which had been erected beside a fast-moving river. They stopped to water Castor and fill their skins. They rode past stone and earth cottages and wooden barns. Before the sun rose, Jakub hid Agata in a hollow of a tree and hobbled Castor beside it so he might graze.

She worried as she waited. Every second the sun moved closer to the horizon. He returned with a man's corpse who smelled of foul wine and a bundle of hay. With an attentive expression, Agata clutched at her cross. Her stomach turned by the smell of dirty flesh, but she desired his blood. Her fangs expanded.

She waited until Jakub saw to Castor's needs. Then she and her husband gorged on the drunk farmer's blood. Once finished, they left the corpse to rot.

*

Chapter 12

CASTOR CARRIED THEM OVER BROKEN ROADS AND through small hamlets where they found shelter and prey. Three weeks later, Jakub and Agata rode into the city of Blois in the twilight and found lodging and stabling. From their window, they could see toward the castle. Built over several centuries, the Château Royal de Blois was comprised of several buildings with different architectural styles. Beneath the stone moldings and lobed arches was an older fortress. The new, Gothic-style entry and main castle featured a large statue of the mounted king above the entrance.

It was hard not to be carried away by exciting thoughts. King Louis XII was a knight, as Jakub was. A warrior king, a king of the people, Louis XII would understand his needs.

With the last of her jewelry, save her wedding ring and rosary, they found a suitable tailor to meet with them.

With the need for blood, but unable to chance poaching a deer, Jakub went hunting for someone who wouldn't be missed. He found a tiny street urchin, hiding against the elements under the eaves of a building. Though he would have preferred a grown hunter or a washerwoman, her pulsing heart was like a song in his ears. It created an agonizing thirst in his soul.

However, he was supposed to be temperate with his eating habits. Was it against the code of Chivalry to harm her?

Before he decided to let her go, he snatched the child

and broke her neck. Whether or not he ate the child or just gave her to Agata, there was no reason to make a child suffer.

Agata said nothing of their meal. With a slack expression and wet eyes, Agata clutched at her cross. She plastered a quivery smile on her lips and then bent down to take a bite out of the dead child. He felt a sharp pain in the back of his throat as he swallowed his remorse.

However, upon seeing Agata drink, Jakub could no longer contain his hunger.

He let his fangs expand and drank her blood. Her flesh was tender — more tender than anything else he had eaten at a vampire. He was a beast, not a knight. This proved it. This was why the vampires roamed, starving in France. They could not quell their hunger.

Agata had her fill and began to weep.

Jakub grew quickly tired of her crying.

How can I love such a woman? Jakub thought without warning. Surprised, he felt lost; his existence was in disarray. *The man I had been is dead. And Agata has become Lamia.* He thought of striking his wife down, cutting off her head and then killing himself and laying them both in the sun.

Forcing his voice to remain low, Jakub growled, "We are reveling in our sins. We are away from God, killing children."

She trembled as his voice rose, but she replied, "I never told you to get a child."

With a bitter smile, he said, "No, but I must hunt while you are safely inside."

"Then, I shall hunt."

"You! You!" Jakub roared. "You are a woman, my wife, and you will not be hunting."

"I could find ... " Agata began.

He cut her off. "I know how you would do it. You would pretend to be a strumpet in order to bring the dogs."

"You pretended I was a strumpet to find our prey in Chilia," Agata snapped.

Exasperation increased in his regret. His hand clenched into a fist. He feared he would strike her, Jakub slammed out of their rented room.

"Where are you going?" Agata asked at the door.

"I need to walk the bear," he snapped and went down the stairs. Thankfully, she did not follow.

He walked to the stables on a pretend task. Every apprentice scooping horse shit, or running errands reminded him of all he had lost. He once knew his place in the world. He once owned an elegant house. He was a father of five— though his children did not know him the way they had known their mother. He once was a noble citizen of Moldovia, but he had killed an innocent child. He would drop the Christian from his name, but his papers referred to him thus. Perhaps he wasn't even the child of Petru any longer. His father was dead. And Jakub was a vampire.

But all that had happened because he left Agata alone to be raped by a vampire and murdered by a priest. If he had been there, he might have protected her. He had failed his lady, his family. He didn't deserve to be a knight.

He walked until the sky lightened and returned to their lodging. Thankfully what was edible on the child had been carved into steaks and what was not had been disposed of. He wanted to apologize to his wife, he wanted to share his pain with her, but he couldn't find the words.

The only words he was able to amass into a semblance of a thought was: "I know you are not a strumpet."

*

Chapter 13

JAKUB ASKED AGATA CUT HIS HAIR TO HIS shoulders as other men — including Louis XII — typically wore. Worse, French fashion dictated he shave off his beard. He had worn a beard and mustache as long as he could grow them. Clean-shaven, he felt even more lost, as if the man he was had drifted even farther away.

He pulled linen shirt over his head and ensured perfect symmetrical gathers at the gold ornamented neckband. Then donned a red velvet collarless doublet cut square and low. His skirted jerkins were tied over the doublet and to that bright satin sleeves. His loose, fur-lined gown opened down the front, with a large turned back collar that broadened over the shoulders. His legs were covered in multiple colored hose, supported by garters.

Jakub did not like the thick French velvets and satin. If de Charny had been alive, Jakub doubted he would like them either. Studying his clothing in the polished mirror (he did not cast a reflection, but his clothes did), Jakub feared something might be used against him: his accent, his Moldavian mannerisms. Agata's accent nearly disappeared under the French, his was always present. And though he understood words when he heard them, speaking was much harder. He planned for obstacles and strategized ways to overcome them, but he hadn't ever been this afraid in battle. He would suffer at his task as long as Agata was safe. Then onto whatever war, the king needed him. And Agata would have a place in society as his wife.

"The carriage is here," Agata said softly.

His beloved wore a round hood over a linen cap and a silk square-necked gown over a kirtle in the French style. The gown had a narrow row of red and black floral embroidery at the neck but was otherwise unadorned. Rubies and diamonds should be set about her throat, but the only jewelry she had left was the amber crucifix and rosary.

Jakub held Agata's hand as they descended the stairs. "My love, I have been fighting wars my entire life, but for this battle, I wish I had Mihai's education."

"Fear not, we shall learn this together." Agata squeezed his hand.

Did that touch mean she had forgiven him his outburst? Jakub hoped so.

With his assistance, she settled into the far cushion of the hired carriage; Jakub sat beside her. The footman pushed the door shut behind with an irritated squeak of the hinges and the thud of wood hitting wood. The leather smelled like moldy bread — no doubt from France's incessant rain.

The carriage carried them up the hill to the Château Royal de Blois's main entrance. Jakub smiled at the statue again.

As they climbed the grand stone staircase, Jakub rubbed his sweaty hands on his clothes. He was glad they chose the red velvet to hide any drips of blood.

The courtiers seem to have a dance in the way that they moved. Yet the dance was unknown to Jakub. He felt clumsy and unsure of himself. Their unending pulses might have driven him mad, if they had not fed on the child.

I am making excuses for my misdeeds, Jakub thought. *I must learn control.*

The soft-spoken French ladies wore heavy skirts of beautiful, brilliant colors. They covered their long hair with French hoods with their caps and billaments decorated with embroidery in a thousand colorful patterns. Their plentiful endowments were hidden by jeweled shawls and exposed by square-cut necklines. While Agata's gray silk seemed plain against the taffeta gowns with embroidered pearls, she was more beautiful than he had ever seen her.

While they waited until it was their turn to seek an audience with the king, Jakub studied everything. Nothing was not as de Charny described, not even the knights.

Jakub was slightly covetous, though the king was a man of forty-eight, there was not a touch of gray in his smooth brown hair that he wore to his shoulders. His steely eyes sat above his falcon's nose. His high cheekbones gave his seemly face a noble bearing.

Jakub noticed how, when Louis stood, he limped ever so slightly. The man had seen several wars. Jakub thought about how before Agata transformed him into a vampire, he too had pains in his back and knees. Yet, in the back of Jakub's mind, he had a strong inclination the king suffered from gout.

Hours went by. The sun moved higher. Jakub's feet and knees ached for the first time since becoming a vampire.

The Franks he had met as allies and as enemies had seemed so eloquent and noble. He had thought that France was a magical, wondrous place, but in many ways, it was more backward than Moldavia had been. There were wars, women in bondage, and starvation among the people, whether they be vampires or humans.

Finally, the herald called out his name.

Jakub and Agata approached the throne.

"Majesty. May I present my wife, Agata, the daughter of Count Artur of the House Vidraru to your queen."

"My lady," the King said with hardly a glance.

The Queen said, "Lady Agata."

Agata did not say anything as she curtsied as the French women. He knew she was listening both to Jakub's conversation with the King and the discussions around the court.

"And how may I assist you?" the King asked.

"You are a man of peace, and you have dealt with your enemies in kind fashion and policy. Your knights, many whom I met on the battlefields in the east, speak of your graciousness." Jakub named a few of the noble knights he worked with during the wars with the Ottoman Empire and Poland, but his words felt clumsy in his mouth. "And I have come to request sanctuary in your lands for my beloved wife and myself. I would forgo hope to join the nobles of the sword."

Jakub passed his references from Voidvode Bogdan and one from his brother and his letters of introduction from the Count of Provence.

"The deputies representing the Second Estate want foreigners to be prohibited from command positions in the military," the king said.

Jakub's dead heart went cold at the new policy. *Did I make a mistake? Will Agata die because I can't protect her.* His face did not leave the King's, but he felt a longing to tear out this King's throat and see his royal blood. Instead, he said, "If not a command position, I heard you require noble horseman in the gendarmerie in the Italian Peninsula. My horse and I have both seen battle."

"Indeed," King Louis said. "Are you Catholic?"

"Yes, Majesty," Jakub said.

"Then I bid you to remain at court, my servants will see to your wife's comfort. I may have something of a man of your talents."

"Thank you, Majesty."

Jakub and Agata backed away to their places in the room.

Then the King spoke to another petitioner who needed help with collecting taxes.

They stood silently in the back of the room listening to the gossip and requests, Jakub learned the rumors he heard from the Count of Providence was correct. The courtiers were concerned with budgetary concerns and reduced pensions. However, Louis XII was more concerned with the lack of a male heir and holding France's hard-won colonies and French expansion into the Italian peninsula. His first queen had been sterile, and rumored disfigured though no one could quite say how.

His second queen had several miscarriages, a stillborn son, and two daughters. King Louis was seeking another queen, but that had nothing to do with Jakub, so he remained silent on the matter and hoped Agata would remain silent on such matters as well.

When the Queen rose to attend the chapel, Agata left with the other women.

Sunlight gleamed against the windows. The glare hurt his eyes. Although, he ached for sleep, Jakub's mind wandered. He wondered if their ancestor was still in the cave, trapped, hungry. Gaius is alone with no one but his demon horse to offer him comfort. But if all that were so, why had he saw him laughing?

Not knowing how or why he drifted away from his body. He felt as if he could see through the cells of his own blood. He saw Agata with the other women, then a dark space of falling ash, and found Gaius astride Nix both hiding under layers of cloth and armor.

"You went with her, stay with her. Let immortality destroy your love," Gaius said to the air.

Jakub tried to back away but found himself stuck, seemingly flying alongside Gaius and Nix.

"I apologize," Jakub whispered, with the hope his body was not doing anything strange in the French courtroom and Gaius would release him from this new bondage quickly. "But I couldn't stay."

"You aren't the first ungrateful offspring, nor will you be the last," Gaius said. "Go to your wife, Jakub, I have an occupation I have set my mind too."

Still not able to return, Jakub asked, "And what is that?"

"Like you, I seek a king."

"To what end?"

"Kings have wars. Wars are good for profit."

"But why am I with you?" Jakub whispered.

"You are my offspring and gifted with the ability to travel through the bloodline." Gaius gave him a knowing look and shook his head. He chuckled. "When you learn to control your gifts, you can find anything you seek better than most. As you dreamed of me, dream of Agata, or better yet yourself, you will find your home again."

Gaius did not lead him astray.

He was back in the courtroom. No one was looking at Jakub or whispering his way. Hopefully, he had not made a fool of himself.

He continued to stand, unmoving. Trying to listen, hoping being surrounded by French accents would help him learn better diction. He thought that though he put a dagger through Gaius's chest, the ancient vampire had just helped him. He simply called him an ungrateful offspring.

It made him think of his elder son, Artur, who had been with Agata when she was attacked in the barn. He had tried to protect her from Nicheola and failed. Jakub regretted that their last conversation was one of casting blame and anger.

✻

THE GRAVEL PATH TO THE CASTLE'S CHAPEL WAS

damp from an earlier storm, but the ladies followed their queen without complaint. Agata wondered if Jakub felt the ache in his feet the way she did. Court was exhausting. At least the layers of clothing and veils protected her from the sun.

Her throat parched, Agata found her bloodlust growing. The Queen and ladies' perfumes mixed with sour breath, sweat, menstrual blood, and the smell of food cooking in the nearby kitchen. Even the jingle of coin and jewelry and purses under clothing and dresses piqued her hunger.

However, every movement, every gesture she made was watched. She was careful to remain with women of her own rank: countesses and count's daughters. Ahead, the women laughed when one made a joke but quieted as they drew closer to the church. Agata caught the distinct sound of the dragging of a rake.

A gardener shoved a rake against the dirty path collecting leaves. His body was covered in a light sweat due to his exertions. She smelled him and heard his regular heartbeat.

The other women's laughter and words fell away. The gardener was the only person in the world. Her prey. She might be able to rush him and take him as he fell to the ground. She would bring her prey to Jakub and show him she could also hunt.

She shook the thought away. She was a foreigner, some minor missteps in etiquette might be tolerated, but not murdering a gardener and drinking blood in front of the Queen.

Agata dipped the fingertips of her right hand in the font of Holy Water beside the entrance to the church. She made the sign of the Cross.

She placed her right knee, lightly and briefly on the ground as she faced the tabernacle. Then she entered the pew beside the other ladies of her rank.

Agata focused on the Holy Mother and said a prayer for her children in broken French so the women would know what she prayed for.

She wished she could help Jakub in some way, but if he was to become a knight of France, this path was the only way. Agata would not speak of her past as a midwife.

Though she wanted to help the Queen, but could not chance becoming embroiled in scandal if this king died without a male heir or divorced her. It was of utmost importance, they prove that they were good Catholics and though they were foreigners understood, accepted, and would assimilate to French culture.

*

Chapter 14

FOR DAYS, JAKUB STOOD AS STILL AS HE COULD, dressed in French court fashion in his place, listening to rumors. Each night he fell into bed and rested in Agata's arms, but neither of them slept well. When they woke, they always found his hair and beard had grown long, and Agata would cut his hair and shave him. They hungered for blood and found it in pigeons and cattle, which held back their thirst, but did not satisfy them. They would not chance killing courtiers or any more commoners — even those who wouldn't be missed.

He feared the waiting would never end. He wondered about Gaius's words: "I seek a king."

One morning after a fortnight, the King's advisor sought him out and asked him to come into the King's bedchamber — a true honor.

Jakub bowed as he entered the bedchamber.

A nobleman shaved the king's face, careful not to nick the royal throat with the razor. Another count brushed off a doublet, nearby.

"At times, I look back with gratification at the expulsion of the English from French soil, but now it is time to expand French interests," Louis said. "As you mentioned, I look to the Italian peninsula."

"Yes, Majesty," Jakub said, forcing excitement back into his stomach.

"However, the Second Estate denies foreigners, no

matter how capable, to oversee our men. Still, I might have an occupation for a man of your talents."

"I shall not fail you, Majesty."

"As you say. My queen tells me your wife is a devout," the King said.

"Indeed, Majesty."

"Yet, she travels beside you."

"My beloved longed to see your beautiful cities and cathedrals. She has a gift with languages; however, my wife has never gone to war with me, nor will she. If you set me upon the Italian Penisula, I ask for her protection."

The king raised an eyebrow. "Is she your beloved? This is the second time you have called her thus."

"Yes, but, Majesty, it was a match between my father and hers to open a trade agreement, but I found I love her and have come to rely upon her good sense."

"A rare gift."

"Thank you, Majesty." Jakub wasn't sure if he spoke of love or a wife with good sense.

"Tell me, why did you come to France? The real reason. You have five children, or so I am told."

At this moment, Jakub knew he must speak plainly. "I was away in battle. My lady was raped by a man who came to steal our cows. Our elder son tried to stop him and suffered injuries. He is, but a lad of fourteen. The priests claimed his sword arm failed due to God's will, but what do priests know of battle? He was outmatched by a full-grown man. Only by God's mercy, my elder daughter is already married, and my youngest was safe with her nurse. Afterward, my brother told me to set Agata aside and hide the shame of our house."

The noblemen seemed aghast, but the king continued his grooming. Jakub waited. So far, he had not been dismissed.

"I love her."

The king's face was wiped with a towel. "I see. Thank

you for your honesty."

"Honesty is a trait which your famed Geoffroi de Charny attributed to all knights, Majesty."

"You know of de Charny?" Louis XII asked.

"Yes, I read his works when I was a lad and why I came to France."

"Indeed, de Charny was a great knight. But do you betray your people, your king, for the love of a woman?"

Moldovia didn't have kings, but this wasn't the time to make the comparison. "I would have never gone to Moldavia's enemies. As my Viovode gave me a recommendation and his blessings to go to France, I do not think he feels betrayed. My brother also understood. My younger nephew fights in the name of our family and my son has taken up my mantle for Viovode Bogdan."

"The same son who failed your lady?"

"The same. But every knight knows the truth, Majesty. My son will face many battles in his life or he will die as any solider. He is brave and noble, his scars carried insight."

Louis XII made a short nod. "As we expand our interests, the Empire has some problematic roads along the countryside which require assistance. Please speak to my Minister of Internal Affairs."

He gestured toward a letter. One of his advisors took the pages with a deep bow. He backed toward Jakub. The men backed out of the chamber together. Then he escorted Jakub to the office of a minister.

The minister took the letter, wrote a few words on it, stamped it with the royal seal, and handed it to Jakub along with copies of three letters from Oliver Cosson Banquier, Count of Limousin.

"Your wife rides beside you?" The advisor said.

"Yes."

"Take care. Count Oliver has one wife in the grave, one wife living, and three mistresses, but not a single son or daughter."

"Not even bastards?" Jakub asked.

"Not even one," the advisor whispered. "And his holdings are large. As our King looks for a wife who can give him a son, so does Count of Limousin."

"Thank you, Sir," Jakub said.

*

Chapter 15

$\mathcal{T}$HE ANCIENT ROAD TO LIMOUSIN WAS PITTED AND holed as other country roads were. Between towns, they passed a few merchant carts, but most had become captives of the cold winter weather. They ate animals that wouldn't be missed: rodents, cats, dogs. They ate the stray human when they could find one alone.

Raindrops fell, incessantly pelting upon and penetrate the long wool cloaks which covered the vampires and protected them from the cold and occasional sunbreak. Icy air stabbed through layers of wet wool and linen. The undead flesh of Agata's hands wrapped around his waist and protected by his cloak felt even colder. The entire countryside smelled damp and musty. The smell of mold, the smell of death. Jakub dreamed of a hot bath, preferably in front of a hearth. He was sure Agata felt the same.

Fearless Castor, his constant friend, slowly walked with his head hung down, his mane dripped from the icy rain. Mud covered his white socks, he looked black from head to hoof. He occasionally snorted, shook his head and slowed to the graze at a stray strand of grass near the road before walking. Jakub did not press the horse on. It was better they moved safely and assuredly through the countryside rather than rush and throw a shoe or twist an ankle.

To distract himself from his discomfort, Jakub thought of the letters which Count Limousin sent to the Crown begging for assistance. They were strangely reticent in detail of the problems plaguing his county. For the last three years, livestock and children around the manor disappeared without a trace. Their people were poor. The loss was making collecting taxes near impossible.

Jakub was to discover what was happening to the people of the county seat of Limousin and bring in the taxes which had been lost.

Though the task was not as Jakub hoped, he found himself with the desire to enjoy this moment. He had found employment in service of the King, he would serve Count Limousin. Even though he was cold, he briefly closed his eyes and drew a deep breath in his nose to allow sweet relief in, but in the back of his mind, he worried.

They rode past the patchwork of fields, somewhere farmers harvested the late crops while others lie fallow. Oxen and sheep grazed the common land. No doubt, all in line with the common plans of the manor.

Jakub rode passed open windows filled with humanity and animal alike. A breadmaker and her cat, no doubt a hard-working mouser. A chandelier. A sculptor and his faithful dog. A stable filled with horses, oxen, mules, and beside it a pen of goats. In another enclosure, chickens clucked, gathering the last few grains before night.

Deeper in town, the blacksmiths were closing shop, tapers, and potters zigzag through the streets carrying their deliveries. A woman leading an ale cart went up the road to the church, a French Gothic structure rising to the heavens.

Outside the town, lay the sprawling manor lands. They rode past an old crumbled château, it's stone returning to Earth. As they drew closer, the ground was littered with broken weapons and rocks.

Jakub wondered why. Many great châteaus were rebuilt after the wars with the English. Perhaps, though Count Limousin's holdings were extensive, over 1200 acres, he had fallen out of the King's favor. After all, a foreign knight was coming to assist him.

"Though now it looks almost idyllic, it looks like once the Château had once been under siege," Agata whispered.

"France has fought in many wars, Sweet Wife. If the Count's family has held the land for generations, no doubt he will tell us the story."

Agata murmured a sound of assent, then she pointed, "Look there!"

Above the treeline, a tower rose in red brick with white stonework built in the Gothic style.

*

THE NEW MANOR WAS SMALLER THAN THE OLD one, and though also in the Gothic style, seemed heavier and squatter than the royal château. It had two towers which rose to heaven, but fewer windows. *Good, that should protect us from the sun,* Jakub thought. *Well it will if this rain ever relents.*

*

TWO MANSERVANTS RUSHED OUT TO MEET THEM. "We heard word, you and your ladyship were coming, Monsuir," The first one said.

Another man came out to take Castor to the stables

Jakub and Agata were brought before Oliver Cosson Banquier, Count of Limousin, a slender man who must be nearing sixty. He had a swirling, mane of silver hair tied with a satin ribbon. Bushy white eyebrows and a dashing well-groomed mustache sprouted from the old man's face.

He swam in his wide-necked satin red doublet under gold jerkin. Thick golden leaves ran up his arms, creating contrasting stripes on his oversized scarlet sleeves. His shirt bore a large frill edged in black at the neck and wide ruffles at the wrist.

On a golden chain, he wore a gold amulet embossed with a large swirling letter B, which danced in the firelight.

Jakub removed his hat and cloak before bowed at the count and then at the countess.

"And may I present my wife, the Lady Agata, Daughter of Count Artur Vidraru."

Though she didn't speak or rise from her bench, Maria Banquier, Countess of Limousin, a woman who looked to be near the same age as Agata, seemed to overpower the room in her conical gown in black edged with white and gold flowers. Her hips artificially widened for fashion. Her braids were covered as the women had been at court, but her brows suggested her hair was also blonde or possibly a light brown. Like the women in court, her painted face was covered in two velvet stars. Presumably covering blemishes, as Agata suggested. As beautiful as she was, Jakub sensed a sadness from her.

If she was as wise as Agata, he would be a fool not to acknowledge her. Jakub bowed and said a few general kindnesses toward the lady.

She replied in kind and then welcomed Agata to her bench. Agata went to her and took her hand. What the ladies spoke about after that Jakub could not hear.

Count Limousin poured Jakub a glass of wine and spoke of business. "I feared the King would send no one. I am thankful you have come though you are a foreign knight, Honorable Petrescu."

"I was pleased with the opportunity, Count Limousin."

"The manor charges a fair banalite for the use of our

mills, but instead of the cens tax, this year, I demanded a portion of ten percent of my vassals' harvests in return for permission to use the land I own. This will be sent to help the war effort on the Italian Peninsula. King Louis is pleased with this arrangement which is why you were sent here. However, the land of this county and road are not important to the King — his wars abroad are his focus. I am so unimportant that he sends a foreign knight to battle my adversaries."

"What adversaries, Count Limousin?"

The count sighed and looked at his hands. They were soft and manicured. Nobles in France were not allowed to plow their own fields. "Once I was a great knight as you are now, somehow I became old. Don't become old, it is quite inconvenient to the laws of Chivalry! You are in your prime, but soon you too will whither."

"Not even the fastest horse can outrun death, Count."

"Indeed." The count said, "Between my great grandfather's service and money, my family became administrators of this land. Long ago, I was injured in battle. I am a man with no son."

Jakub nodded in understanding, but he knew the man did not want him to speak.

"I can't work the land and keep my title, but the land withers. You are a chevalier without land, without title in this country. She has given you children?"

"Yes. Five. The eldest is going to be a mother herself soon."

"Sons?"

"Two."

He nodded and sighed again.

"Who are your enemies, my Count?"

"My township and lands wither due to three witches that live in a glen. They have a legion on brigands who hunt along our trade road. I have a gendarmery at my command, they are not true warriors.

"They are not battle-tested and have no stomach for it. I, myself, am old. Kill them for me and I shall call you son. As my son you will inherit this land in perpetuity for your sons and their sons, better than my damned nephew who haven't seen so much as a winter's chill. He would squander the inheritance."

Jakub's heart felt as if it skipped a beat, then froze solid. He had seen too often inconvenient women called witches. He tried to come up with an excuse, but he was a noble warrior.

Trying to stall he said, "That is beyond generous, but I am still a foreigner."

The Count said, "If the King denies this, then we can buy an office from the King. I must be generous because the task at hand is most vile — and many others have failed."

"Buy an office?" Jakub asked, growing more disillusioned by France with every word.

"The new generation are vastly different than those who lived previously. Our culture has moved toward the secular. The crown has noble titles for sale, even though merchants and their ilk care not for the divine right of the King. They care for money and comforts," the count said.

"I think we all care for comforts to a certain degree," Jakub said. "Not for ourselves, but for our wives. How will I find these witches?"

"They are led by Deifrida Millet, the other two are Adelina and Iuletta. One of them has had a babe. That's why my men didn't kill them before. They live in the glade near a moss-covered carved megalith. It is there they sacrifice children to Satan."

"They sacrifice children to Satan?" Jakub was sure now the women weren't witches, but he could not show his internal conflict.

"How else can we explain all those we lost?" the count

said. It wasn't a question.

"And Agata will be safe here 'til I return?"

"Of course, she's in my hospitality and protection."

"Thank you, Count Limousin."

"Now you must be hungry and tired from your journey, my wife has already seen to your comfort.

Your rooms are ready, and there is water to bathe yourselves."

✴

JAKUB ENTERED AGATA'S BEDCHAMBER WITH A determination in his step. Seeing the maid, a young girl of fifteen or sixteen, who ran a comb through her long raven hair. He said in Moldavian: "Tell her to leave."

"Leave us," Agata told the girl, who curtsied and left. Yet he did not doubt the maid would listen at the door and report what was said to the count or countess. He gestured for her to continue in Moldavian.

Agata untied the lashings, which held the layers of fabric in place until she wore only a chemise.

Jakub sharpened his sword. "The count has asked me to kill witches. You know as well as I, the chances are these witches are just midwives or someone else otherwise inconvenient. Did you tell anyone here you practice midwifery?"

"No, my love. We spoke of our journey to France. I told her we both got quite seasick and that I missed our children and hope to be reunited one day, though our eldest son lives well and runs our estate."

"Good. Take care of your words until I return. You must not be inconvenient to the count or his wife. These people are not what I expected."

"Why do you fret so?" she asked.

"These people are backward. So, speak of nothing unless you want to be burned at the stake or strung up to a tree."

"Perhaps, I might come with you. You will be dealing with women and my conversational French is cleaner than yours."

Jakub collected his thoughts as he moved precisely and organized his gear. He scabbarded his newly sharpened blade. After fighting for princes who changed allies even in the middle of wars, Jakub learned long ago, he must be flexible with the rules of engagement. Unorthodox thinking and humility above all else were one of the reasons he walked away from battles that others had not.

"Very well, my lady, you will walk beside me, but you must do what I say and retreat when I tell you to retreat."

"Yes, my husband."

"And if our foes grow too numerous, I wish for you to return to this place. It is not a perfect sanctuary, but does offer some protections and comforts," Jakub said.

*

Chapter 17

AGATA CLUTCHED JAKUB AROUND THE WAIST AS they rode through the formal garden with its neat hedgerows. The stone path became a sunken dirt trail as they passed the beehives, and the fruit orchard became a wild forest of oak, beech, and ash trees. With every step, civilization seemed farther away. She hoped these witches were just wise women as she once had been. Happy he agreed to take her, Agata refused to whine about him her fright. She wanted to be brave for her husband, but it was logical that if vampires existed, then witches existed as well.

Whether they be witches or just wise women, perhaps I might learn French remedies and become a beloved lady again. This thought soothed her nerves.

Three miles from town, they passed the carved, moss-covered megalith and found a small wooden lean-to hut, just where the count had told Jakub it would be.

An elderly woman and two young girls — the older one looked to be twelve or thirteen and younger five or six — cleaned and shelled beans. A woman in her prime chopped firewood with a small hatchet.

The women wore their wool tunics to mid-calf over a longer tunic which was most likely made from hemp. The younger had her tunic tucked into her belt. Their feet were clad in loose leather. Like other married women of France, their hair was covered in a veil held by a ribbon of the same wool as their tunics. The older woman had a simple shawl made of what looked like goatskin over her shoulders. The younger, most likely warmed due to her exertions, wore no outer garment. Sweat stained her undertunic.

The children's tunics were slightly shorter, and their feet were bare. The younger looked up, her light brown hair floating in the breeze. Agata thought of Daciana. She would have had her fifth birthday by now.

Deifrida snapped, "Iuletta, take Joia inside."

That was Iuletta? A girl? Agata felt a pain in the back of her throat. Witch or not, she did not want to see Jakub murder a child.

The elder picked up the bucket of beans and tried to take her sister's hand.

The little one tried to protest, but, ahead of her grandmother's swat, the younger girl ran into the cabin.

"Who's there?" the older woman called. "Show yourself, Devil, or my daughter-in-law will send you to meet your maker.

Jakub led Castor before the women. The women glanced at him and then up at Agata. She knew they were witches. Real witches.

Dear God, let Jakub be merciful ...

✳

JAKUB SAW AGATA'S GLANCE TOWARD THE HEAVENS and press her hands to her breastbone. He did not need his wife to speak to see the girls' presence had upset her. Jakub sensed the younger woman tense her small hands around her ax.

"You are the witch, Deifrida?" Jakub asked the old woman, but he did not draw his sword or make any move toward violence. He kept his hands in front of him.

"I am Deifrida, pilgrim. But I am no witch, who in God's name, are you, foreigner, and your lady?" The old woman replied.

"I am Sir Jakub, Son of the late Count Petru, brother to Count Mihai, this is my wife, the Lady Agata, daughter of Count Artur Viradu, sister to another count named for his father."

The two women glanced at each other.

The younger one curtsied. The older one only inclined her head.

"We were told witches roamed the land and caused mischief; Jakub was told to find you," Agata said in French.

"What's it to you, foreigner? Are you one of the damned inquisitors? We swear on the good book, we are Catholics."

"No, I am not an inquisitor. I was charged to clean the road of its troubles to bring trade to the village by the king's orders," Jakub switched to Moldavian. Agata translated.

"I am sure the King knows nothing of us — though I gave my husband and son to his war. My daughter-in-law, Adelina, gave her husband, the girls gave their father. Haven't we paid enough?"

"We came ... "

Deifrida wasn't finished. "Joia never even met her father. Poor Iuettta weeps for him to come home."

Even before Agata translated, Jakub felt a slight tremble in his hand. He had killed women before. All on the battlefield died from the sword, but he didn't want to hurt four women in a little hovel. His heart ached for the little girl who never knew her father. His youngest hadn't really known him either.

"Are you midwives?" Agata asked from Castor's back. Jakub sensed she was careful that her voice did not crack in pain or fear.

"No, milady. We make soap from the moss in the forest,"

Deifrida said. "And the slime of the beast."

"Know why someone would call you a witch?" Jakub asked.

"Because people don't like widows and fatherless babes, no matter how we try to protect them from the beast."

"Protect them?" Agata asked.

"Milady and Milord, there is a beast in the wood, which, if we speak of will seem inconceivable. There must not be many of them, but I have never heard that one had been caught or found dead.

"We don't like to speak of it, lest you think we are mad. But we are not mad. The creature exists. I swear it on your good lady's holy cross, milord," Deifrida said.

"What is the beast?" Agata asked.

"We don't know exactly, perhaps some giant snake. It lives under the ground , deep in the caverns to the south, and snatches children and livestock caught unaware," Adelina said. "Iuletta, bring us a jar of slime."

The elder girl did as her mother bade.

"But it makes this slime which we put in our soap," Iuletta said.

The story that the witches told Agata seemed so fantastic, Jakub wasn't sure if Agata's broken French was sufficient, but he chose to trust the women. He knew they were telling the truth.

"We can't catch it on our own, but we can tell you to avoid being scented by the beast is paramount when surviving with it," Deifrida said.

"We smell like it, so it doesn't smell us. That is how we survive living in the wood," the younger girl, Joia, said from the window.

"If people weren't so ignorant, they'd survive too, but they don't want to smell like our soap," Adelina said.

"We were chased out of the village when we thought to rub the slime on the door frames so it would pass over us, just like the blood and the angels in the Good Book."

"Why don't you leave?"

"And go where? At least here, we are left unravaged, but what of my daughters? The road is dangerous and expensive."

Jakub nodded. He didn't know if the creature the Millet women described had a nose, but like other large game, the greatest obstacle to cornering and defeating the beast would be beating its nose or other smelling apparatus.

"I have no wish to kill innocent women, so I shall seek this beast out. I hope for your sake you speak the truth.

"Come, my lady, I'll take you home."

Deifrida pressed a large bar of soap into Jakub's gloved hands. "Take the soap, it will protect you. And you lady? Take the soap and wipe it on you and your house."

Jakub glanced up at Agata. Her brow had risen to a concerned point. He fished in his saddlebag for payment. He gave them a single gold coin, a loaf of bread, and dried mutton for their time and the soap.

"If Jakub falls, then you must run for your daughters' sake," Agata warned them.

✳

Dear Irina,

I hope this missive finds you well.

Your honored father and I might have found a home. There is a great evil here that he must vanquish. I pray to God for his victory and the health of you and your newborn child.

We are staying with the kind Count and his gentle wife of Limousin.

Please write to me and tell me how you fare and if the child is a boy or a girl. And tell me how Daciana, Artur, and Petru fare.

With all my love,
Mother

On the next page was another recipe. This one called Sun-Preserved Venison was a coded description of how Jakub carved the vampires and left them to burn in the daylight.

*

Chapter 18

CHE COUNT LIMOUSIN HAD A LIGHTNESS TO HIS steps as he and a servant hurried down to meet Jakub and Agata. Jakub liked him less for it. Even if they were witches, there was no need to enjoy the killing of four helpless women.

"The witches have met their doom?" the Count said.

"No. There is a bigger problem than witches," Jakub said dismounting.

Count Oliver's expression went hard. "A bigger problem? So, you will fail me?"

Once Jakub helped Agata off Castor's back, he spoke: "The women are just poor widows, uncouth and unkempt, yes, but women who lost their husbands in the King's war in the Italian Peninsula."

"They are trying to protect the town with their remedies, not cause suffering," Agata said. Jakub noticed how careful she was to not use the word witches.

"Perhaps, Lady, you think you ought to give them comfort," the count said. "But we burn heretics in France."

Agata looked to the ground. "Forgive me, Count Oliver." But Jakub could see Agata was already playing the part of a dutiful and obedient daughter-in-law to Oliver, wife to Jakub.

"Before I kill any women, I must see the truth in their crimes. I will see your magistrate."

"You put the lives of three witches above a chance to be a knight?"

"A noble name is nothing without a noble purpose," Jakub said.

"Young people!" Count Oliver said. (Though it had been many years since Jakub could call himself young.) "Very well, off with you."

*

JAKUB LET CASTOR RUN DOWN THE DIRT ROAD between the manor and the town. Agata held on tightly to his waist. As the horse galloped, Jakub did feel young. Free. He had made the right decision in not killing the Millet women.

The horse slowed as they entered the town.

Two monks walked side by side. Jakub scowled at their dirty clothes and lice-filled hair.

"God be with you," they called out. "But shouldn't … "

Jakub ignored them. Castor snorted.

In Moldavia, it was considered a wickedness not to marry and have children even among most priests, but here in France many men lived in solitude with other men as monks.

That was not a life of adventure and daring. He cared not what they claimed was a sin: especially in regard to Agata.

They stopped at the town hall and went inside.

The mayor and the magistrate welcomed Agata and Jakub into the town hall with their mouths; their eyes held suspicion, but their wrinkled faces exposed that these men wanted what the count wanted. It was good for all of them.

"When did the town first notice the disappearance?" Jakub asked the magistrate.

"Well, let's see," The magistrate took out a large tome. He blew a cloud of dust off the old volume, then he opened it his fingers turned the vellum carefully as he ran a finger along a column of dates. These attacks always start in the spring and end after the first frost.

1508:
21/04: Missing goat reported
05/05: Missing goat reported
09/06: Missing goat reported
12/07: Missing goat reported
19/07: Brigands were seen on the road. Three men, one woman.
18/08: Missing pig reported in the summer pasture.
19/08: Iean Val reported missing while searching for loss pig
17/09: Missing goat reported
3/10: Missing goat reported
26/10: Missing cow

"This does not say anyone was anyone attacked by the brigands?" Jakub asked.

"No, it doesn't." He turned the page.

"Not very masterful brigands," Agata said. "Was anyone brought in?"

"No, they seem to have disappeared or moved on to more profitable roads, but of course, no one would report that," the magistrate said.

"Then why does the Count believe the brigands still disturb the road?" Jakub asked.

"Because we have no better answer," the magistrate said in exasperation.

"Even if the Millet women were stealing all this livestock, certainly they couldn't use it all," Jakub said.

"At least for no Christian purpose," the magistrate said.

They looked over the reports for 1509. They were similar. Starting in the spring and ending in the fall, several goats, cows, and children were reported missing.

In 1510, more of the same. Except after two children disappeared, there was a "public disturbance."

"What does that mean?" Jakub asked.

"Well, you see, the public blamed the witches and chased them from the town."

"But look, before it, two children, six goats, and a cow go missing. This is people's future we are talking about."

Obviously growing irritated, since she knew she should be silent in front of the other men.

Magistrate looked at Jakub, who growled out: "Answer the lady's question."

"According to this, it looks like right after the town built the new well."

"How deep is as well?"

"Near a hundred feet. We had to go deep. Our former well was tainted with the plague. The English."

"So, it may be a beast which lives in the Earth," Agata said thoughtfully. "Do you have a Bestiary at your disposal?"

"No, my lady, but I'll call on the mayor. His brother is a man of great learning. Boy!" the magistrate shouted. "Get this to the mayor."

"What is it that you seek, my lady?" Jakub asked.

"Some creatures can only be killed by poison. Some can only be destroyed by fire, my love, I cannot ride into battle with you, but I shall help any way I can.

The boy returned with a youngish man — the mayor's brother — holding his book as if it was a sacred treasure.

"I wasn't sure you could read."

"French is not our first language, so I accept any help you give, good sir," Agata said.

Soon she had pushed the mayor's brother away from his book as she poured through the bestiary: looking for serpents, giant worms, and other creatures of the underground.

To distract the men from his wife's task, he asked for more information about the era.

✳

AGATA HAD BEEN SITTING IN ONE POSITION FOR A few hours when she noticed the men were speaking softly by the fire. She turned the final page and went back to each scrap of paper in which she marked pages and reread each description.

Basilisks were a possibility, as they lived in deep caves. However, they turned their victims to stone. Statues of children and livestock suddenly appearing and dotting the countryside would have been remembered.

Giant worms burrowed with gaping maws through solid rock for prey and some are known to have stingers on their tails, but those were more often seen in the mountains.

La Guivere were serpents with horns sprouting from its forehead known to attack without provocation.

Lou Carcolh was a giant mollusk with tentacles that burrowed through the ground to strike prey. They were known to leave trails of slime.

This must be it!

"Jakub, I believe you may be facing Lou Carhol," Agata said. "Unfortunately, my love, there is no known way to kill the beast."

"Lou Carhol has not been seen for an age in these parts!" the mayor's brother said.

"I also wondered about La Guivere, but they don't

leave a trail of slime," Agata said. "Logic dictates a beast so large, but unseen is wise and more deliberate in their actions."

"I should say just the fact it existed for centuries, tells us that," the mayor's brother said with a huff.

✳

"INEED A CART AND A MAN AT ARMS TO DRIVE IT," Jakub said to the Count's company of men. This was no job for Castor. He was not charging into battle. He was exterminating a beast.

For a moment, the men just looked at each other. There were grumbles about working for this stranger who has come among them.

"Milord, I would volunteer if it pleases you." a young man, perhaps of nineteen or twenty, said quickly. Timothé de Carron was a dark-haired man who, even between shaves, did not have a full beard. His frame still held the lankiness of youth under his leathers, but his eyes looked upon Jakub as if he saw something sacred.

"Your rank, good sir?"

"Gendarme. I am capable with both the lance and the bow, my lord." Timothé paused and said, "And I am the younger son, my lord."

A gendarme, a noble-born man at arms. And he was the younger, more expendable son of a landed knight. As Jakub was the younger, more expendable son of a count, he understood Timothé's wish to prove himself. The lad was hiding his frustration at his station in the small, quiet corner of France.

"And your captain gives his blessings?" Jakub asked.

"He will if you request me, my lord."

"Can you drive a cart as well as ride?"

"Yes, my lord."

"Are you married, sir?" Jakub asked. He did not want a man to see his doom before he lived at least a little.

"Yes."

"And your wife?"

"Is here in the castle with our babe and pregnant with our second," Timothé said.

"Excellent. Timothé deCarron walk with me," Jakub said.

The younger man fell into step, and the two moved to the armory.

"Are we going to kill the witches, milord?" Timothé asked.

"We are going to kill a bigger beast than that."

"I never saw the beast, but I've seen the witches," Timothé said in disappointment.

"Killing women is nothing; do you want fake glory or your name to live on forever?"

Timothé's young face lit up in excitement. "What are we going to do first?"

"First, I need a strong ox or cart horse and a cart. Then we both need armaments. See to it."

"Yes, milord," Timothé said.

Watching the younger man scurry to his tasks, Jakub rubbed the back of his neck and stretched though the routine soreness had disappeared.

He went to the stables. "This is no place for a charger, Castor, you will be remain here," he said, giving his horse a pat. "But Agata or the stable boy will ride you once a day for exercise and brush you. We'll be reunited soon."

If Banquier would name him son, then he would be Jakub Banquier and would inherit Limonsin. It wasn't what he hoped for, but it would give them a place.

✱

Chapter 19

"**B**E WELL, AND BE SAFE, MY LOVE." AGATA TIED AN embroidered ribbon to his arm as the French ladies were known to do. "This quest will take all of your senses to succeed, but I believe you will."

Though the Count and Countess watched, she kissed him on the lips. Not a nobleman in several countries could claim a wife like Agata.

Emboldened, Timothé's wife, a girl no older than Irina, said goodbye in the same manner.

Agata and Madame deCarron waved goodbye with tears in their eyes. Driving the cart pulled by a brown mare named Buttercup, Jakub and Timothé rode away from the village. Timothé stretched his back and took a deep breath. Jakub noticed how the mist leaving the gendarme's mouth was more substantial than his own, he would have to be careful.

"Tired?"

"Yes, my lord. Apologies. But I am ready for action."

Jakub got an inkling the other man was happy to be leaving the château.

"And your family is well?"

"Baby was up all night with the colic. My good wife was up pacing with her all the while our son was kicking her. A strong boy will be a nice change."

"My firstborn was a daughter, too," Jakub said. "Then a boy, then a girl, then another boy and another girl. They all cried.

And they all favored my lady when they were small. "As a babe's needs defeat that of any warrior, I must say I also looked toward battle at times. However, you and I, Timothé, look toward a battle we can win." Jakub took a skin of watered wine and handed it to the man at arms. "To your lady's health and the health of your two babes."

"Thank you, my lord."

Buttercup neighed as if in agreement.

✳

JAKUB RODE BESIDE TIMOTHÉ ON THE CART BACK to Deifrida's hovel. Timothé held his breath and crossed himself once he spotted the Millet women who, like before, shuffled the girls back into their hovel. Jakub jumped down from the cart and said, "Hail, good women."

"You've returned," Deifrida said.

"I, along with my beloved wife, have gotten the community to believe in the beast," he told the two women "Now, this man and I hunt it. First, we wish you to anoint this cart and horse and us with your soap. And tell us anything you know."

The women did what was asked and then gestured the men to follow them deeper into the wood.

"The one thing we know for sure is that this spiraling trail shows a place where the beast has traveled," Deifrida said. She pushed branches out of the way until she showed them a spiraling pattern in the dirt which ended in a hole which spanned the width of Jakub's hand.

"Good we didn't bring the horse, likely to break a leg," Timothé said.

"These holes are a sign the trail is fresh," Adelia

said. "When they are older they fill in with worms and leaves from the trees."

"Big, old beasts learn and adjust. You must do the same," Deifrida said.

That all seems simple, doesn't it? Jakub thought. *Track the beast, become a childless man's son, and get Agata a place in society.*

"It would be best all-around if you traveled under cover of darkness, Sir," Deifrida said. Suddenly Jakub wasn't sure the wise old woman wasn't more than a woman. He quickly decided, *As long as she lived by the laws of the land, it doesn't matter.*

With the Millet womens' advice, he and Timothé tracked the beast for two nights deeper into the weir. As the trees grew thick; the men found more slimy holes filled with worms. Then Jakub discovered a swirling track broken by several holes on the end of a long finger of woods.

Timothé remained with the cart and Buttercup.

Doing his best to not leave too much of his scent too close, Jakub walked two paces beside the trail to see where it led. He found a wetland with thick cover. The signs disappeared under the murky water, but there was a high ground that looked to be the perfect vantage point. Except Jakub had hunted both man and beast too often to know ideal vantage points, does not guarantee success.

He returned to Timothé.

They gathered their gear and, holding it above their heads, waded out to the small patch of ground.

The men set up a makeshift camp. They hung a tarp and covered it with moss to create a blind to limit the beast's knowledge of their movements. Flies buzzed about and bit Timothé, who slapped them away. Occasionally, Jakub pretended to slap them away from himself.

He felt they caused too much commotion with all their movements and he wondered if Timothé's pulse was as loud to the beast as it was to him.

*

Chapter 20

Agata was in a deep sleep when she was summoned to the parlor. Though the sun was up, she knew better to keep the countess waiting. She dressed as formally as her limited wardrobe would allow. Meeting her hostess in the parlor was undesirable. If Countess Banquier wanted to be bosom companions or even friends, she would have met Agata in her bedroom.

Maria, Countess Banquier, was no doubt adored by the male sex for her flowing golden hair, which lay braided and covered. Her imperious nose and angular cheekbones might look masculine, except they tapered down to her soft jaw. Her brown eyes darted toward the door, agleam with emotion. "You often sleep during the day." Her crescent moon eyebrows rose as if her statement was a question, but it was an accusation.

"Yes, I find myself exhausted from our recent excursions," Agata replied.

"Perhaps I ought to call a midwife?" Maria handed Agata a flagon of wine.

Agata wanted to say: "I am a midwife," instead she said, "There is no need, Countess, though I thank you for your concern."

Maria took a large gulp of wine. This was also a bad sign. "Would you steal my home from me?" Her perfectly manicured nails tapped on the wooden top of a small table on which she set her cup.

"No, Countess," Agata said.

Maria's heart beat faster. The elevated pulse clouded Agata's vision of the woman in front of her.

"You think you might be the mistress of this estate and cast me out? You. The foreign wife of a foreign knight errant will never be mistress of this estate."

"No, Lady Banquier," Agata said.

Maria rose to her feet and grabbed Agata's wrist. She squeezed tightly. This close, Agata could see the pulse under her throat. She wanted to open that delicate throat and drink.

Looking at the pain on the Countess's face, she wondered if Jakub would leave her, perhaps not now, but in the centuries to come. How often women's happiness is based either on the men that they are married to or their children. Agata had lost her children when she became this damnable thing.

"You wrote your daughter this letter!" The unsent letter sat on Lady Banquier's table.

Thankfully, there was nothing of their condition in it even in code, but Agata hoped Irina was well.

Maria's eyes grew wider. "Are you with child? Do not mock me!"

Agata now knew Maria meant to kill anyone who stood in her way. She cried, "No. But I promise you this. If Jakub succeeds, you will not be cast out. You shall be his stepmother after all."

Maria's face grew ugly as fury twisted her lips into a sneer. She lifted a small knife from under her skirt and dashed toward Agata.

Agata sidestepped away from the blade.

Agata wished she knew more vampire powers. Perhaps she should have stayed in Moldavia to learn them

"Countess, if Jakub succeeds, we were going to ask for the old chateau. We wanted to rebuild it." She hoped she was dominating Maria's mind, but she wasn't sure.

Maria dropped the knife. It clattered on the wooden floor. She sank down into a chair and began to weep into her hands.

Agata kicked the knife across the room.

"Did you marry for love?" Maria whispered between sobs.

"No, our fathers wanted to solidify a contract."

"You are so lucky to have not been married to an old man. I have been married for fifteen years and have not carried a child to term. It is his seed. I know it is."

"Has he ever had a bastard?"

"No. Not a one."

"Yet, still, the women are always blamed," Agata said. "It is the same everywhere."

Maria nodded dully. At that moment, she knew she had dominated the other woman's mind.

Agata and Maria walked into the Countess's private chamber. The carved bed looked snug enough, but Agata was shocked to see the lack of comforts. Her own room had a woven rug on the floor, but Maria's was simply bare wood.

"We might be sisters, you and I," Agata said softly and drew closer.

Maria's eyes were bloodshot from crying, but she rose her head. "I'll call the guards if you don't leave."

Not entirely dominated then.

"No, you will protect my husband, your only son," Agata said.

"Why?"

"Because, if you follow your end of this bargain, he and I shall care for you greater than any natural-born son. You will remain mistress of this house and advisor to the new count, Good Countess. Unlike your husband, Jakub will never deny you any liberty. If you wish to remarry, for love, you may do so."

"What are the promises of his wife?"

"I am noble-born. I give my oath upon my noble blood. Look into my eyes and see I speak the truth."

Agata tried to push the vision into Maria's mind. She did not know if she was succeeding. Seconds ticked by. There was no answer, but Maria had not screamed either.

Agata sunk her teeth into the Countess's throat. Careful not to take too much, she sipped the blood. Maria's skin grew paler, but her heart remained strong. Agata pressed a handkerchief onto the wound, kissed her, and tucked her under her blankets.

"I protect my new son," Maria said in a deadened voice.

And we shall protect you and offer you every comfort after your husband passes from this world, she thought to Maria.

"Make it quick," Maria said before she fell asleep.

"You will have only sweet dreams of Jakub and I, of friends and of comfort in your dotage," Agata whispered.

Exhausted, she left the countess and went into the count's study. "Hail, my lady, Agata."

"Hello, Count Oliver. I ask you to mail this letter to my child in Moldavia. Apparently, it was waylaid. You may read it if you so desire. You will find it speaks highly of you and your dear wife."

The count pressed Agata toward the fireplace. No matter what he claimed, he was never a knight. Not like Jakub.

"Will you not go to your wife's room tonight?"

"For what purpose?"

"You seem to still want a natural-born son rather than an embraced one," Agata said.

"I might try for a bastard," he said with a lecherous

smile.

"Then, my count, you ought to sleep."

The count yawned.

It was working! And this time much faster.

"Perhaps I might call for wine?" Agata said.

"Wine would be good." He yawned again.

She rang the bell and called for the wine. She ensured this time the count told the steward to mail the letter at the inn.

Perhaps, Agata thought to herself, *This loneliness is why the legends speak of vampires existing away from God. We exist with the remorse of many lifetimes.*

✳

Chapter 21

A COLDNESS PASSED OVER JAKUB AS HE SAT IN THE muck, waiting for a sign of the beast, listening to the heartbeat of his man at arms and the cart horse Buttercup who was back on the road.

He thought of Gaius bleeding in the cave, his pugio sticking out of his chest. *The great general who made a covenant with the nobility that lasted a thousand years at least. The great warrior who my wife defeated. And I didn't even make a killing blow.*

Jakub wondered if this regret would ever pass or if it was eternal as he was eternal.

Perhaps that is why the legends speak of vampires existing away from God. We live with the regret of many lifetimes, rather than just one.

Coated in a shimmering slime, a giant serpent, its underbelly covered in suckers, and slithered through the underbrush. Searching, it pressed blades of grass and branches out of its way. Occasionally it broke a twig.

"Look there!" Jakub whispered.

"My lord, it is as large as we assumed," Timothé whispered in awe.

Watching the creature's movement, Jakub was sure its weight was not on the limb. That must mean there is more of the beast, somewhere. Just as Agata's description had said.

"And that's just the limb?" Jakub said.

"A limb?" Timothé repeated, rather dumbly. Then his face paled with understanding.

Jakub threw a deer shank toward the slithering limb. When it hit the grass, the tentacle hastened toward the vibration. Jakub could still not see where the tentacle ended. It wrapped itself around the deer shank and swung it side to side as if trying to snap the neck of its prey.

Jakub leaped from his blind with his saber in his right hand, the dagger in his left. He stabbed the tentacle who pulled at the bloody deer flesh. The smell of rancid old algae rotting on a scorching day filled Jakub's nostrils. The appendage jerked backward and circled around the meat again. It grabbed hold and retracted into the wet earth.

Jakub and Timothé hunted for the creature, watching movement under the ground until they came to a wet grotto. Inside they could hear shifting and slithering. They had found its lair.

*

Chapter 22

AGATA SPREAD THE WITCHES' SOAP ONTO HER clothing in the hope that it worked as they claimed and climbed out her window.

The garden paths divided into four separate walks to enjoy the vistas in each direction. The western route passed the main pastures and stables. Quiet now with the horses and cows in the barn for the night. She crossed under a large shrub of blooming blackthorn and saw three does dash away across the meadow, now a blanket of spring flowers: violets, bleeding hearts, and lily-of-the-valley. She walked on to the forest glade, full of deep-rooted oaks, beech, and ash trees which bore witness to times past. *It's so beautiful, and one night, I shall be its mistress.*

Agata traced the path through the grove to the ancient megaliths. Chamomile, dill, rosemary, and other herbs trembled in the night breeze concealing yet drawing attention to the small lean-to. Inside, the child argued about going to bed.

Agata's heart ached for her own children, but her eyes alighted upon two rabbit carcasses draining into a trough. She knocked on the heavy red door.

The old witch peeked out of the small window.

"Hello, Madame. Do you remember me?" Agata asked.

"How may we serve you, undead lady?"

"You know me?" Agata asked.

The old witch smiled and gestured toward the rabbits. "And we knew you would come. For your refreshment, my lady."

The old witch passed her a cup. Once, Agata had her fill, the old woman opened her door and motioned for her to enter.

Inside, the room was clean, Agata felt the oppressive nature immediately of the small cabin. Ample wooden cupboards filled with ceramic jars of organs, eyeballs. Empty beakers, scales, and ceramics of all shapes and sizes lined the east wall.

She forced a smile to her face. She sat in the chair which the woman offered. "Why do you pretend you aren't a witch?"

"Why do you pretend you aren't a vampire?" Deifrida said.

"Society deems us evil."

"They deem us evil as well."

Deifrida set out bread studded with currants and put a pot of herbal tea over the fire. Agata did not partake in the bread but did take a sip of chamomile tea.

"Like you, I know the healing arts — I was going to offer a trade. Your knowledge of local plants to mine for the healing arts of Moldavia?" Agata suggested.

A shadow of desolation drifted onto the younger witch's face, but it disappeared quickly as her mother-in-law turned to her.

"We need your society more than knowledge," the old witch said.

Agata would have never guessed the witches might be lonely. "I, too, walk alone with only Jakub as my companion."

"And the countess?"

"Believes I want to kick her out of her house."

"If she would invite us — even to a fate — we would be reinstated in the village."

"I shall do what I can, but I can't guarantee an invitation … But as it might be many years until I am mistress of the house, perhaps I could hire your elder daughter as my maid. It will also put her near the townsfolk. Then, at Easter, I could invite you all. The count could not deny my maid's family at the spring party."

"Then we'll share our knowledge with you, Lady Agata," Deifrida said.

*

VISCOUS SLIME COVERED THE OPENING TO THE cave. The entrance was small, Jakub squeezed inside, Timothé close behind. Dawn's light spilled inside, Jakub could see nothing more than mucky soil and vegetable debris litter the floor.

Timothé's heartbeat echoed in Jakub's ears, but otherwise, the lack of sound reminded Jakub of the silence after a battle. He enjoyed such moments.

Sheltered in the earth and enveloped by darkness, Jakub felt at home for the first time since landing in France. As they moved deeper, his nostrils were filled with a musty, brackish smell. Beyond the next turn, he heard water dripping and hitting a small pond or puddle.

This dark, musty place was home. He removed his glove and scooped a handful of dirt into a bag. He felt the earth between his fingers and knew the comfort that Agata knew from her crock of garden soil.

The tunnel curved; darkness became complete.

"We dare not go further, milord," Timothé said.

"I do dare." He lit a candle and stuck it in the dirt. The candlelight bounced off the glittering, slime-covered walls.

"I can barely see even with the candle, milord."

Yet Jakub could see outlines of boulders and rocks. Perhaps, only a vampire might kill this beast for the darkness of the cave was complete. *If that was the case, then did God give me the opportunity to be a vampire to slay this beast?* Jakub didn't like the thought, because it's logical conclusion was God allowed Agata to be raped and murdered. *And if God could be that cruel then I would kill Him if I get the chance.*

Jakub's foot stepped on something which snapped. He knew it was not a stick. He looked down and found the bones of animals and humans. Fractured fence posts and hewn boards and bundles of straw littered the floor of the cave.

"Oh, dear God," Timothé breathed.

"Indeed," Jakub said. "Perhaps, once such a massive terror itself would have been venerated as a God."

Peering out of a spiraling shell of brilliant spirals of indigo, violet, and magenta was a mass of globular flesh with two eyes and a large pointed beak. When it opened its mouth to taste the bloody wound at the end of the tentacle, the creature's gut-wrenching breath smelled like rotten eggs and algae.

Jakub threw pieces of deer toward it.

It took the bait. As it pulled the flesh of the deer toward its mouth, Jakub witnessed how viscous saliva pooled between its rows of teeth and spilled onto the earth upon the ground among its own glutinous slime. As Agata had warned, the creature's gaping mouth was surrounded by several long, hairy, and slime-covered tentacles that extended outward though not for miles. These appendages stretched out from the cave it inhabited for a long distance and dragged victims back to its abode.

Rows of hard teeth scraped the flesh off the carcass before clamping its gigantic mouth shut on the entire thing. On its head, it bore four retractile tentacles. The lower pair shorter and the upper longer and on its chest were even longer tentacles.

Fleshy folds of skin, like the smaller snails Jakub had seen, it moved on one foot.

Jakub felt both excited and horrified by the grotesque scourge. Its very existence meant something. He was no longer just a cavalry officer in a battle against men. This was his moment to become who he indeed was: a knight sent on a quest to defeat a mighty beast.

He wondered if Saint George felt this way when he first saw the dragon. Then he laughed at the thought.

A tentacle reached for him, but with a celerity, he never knew in life, he stepped back toward the wall. It reached for Timothé, who shouted. His saber blade sliced through the slimy flesh.

Another appendage turned in time to back away from his swing. It parried and swung wildly. This must be a somewhat intelligent creature. Agata had been correct about that too.

Amid this horrific numbness, the beast roared. It was a roar that could shake the foundations of the earth if there was such a thing.

Unfeelingness, coldness surrounded him. He heard splashing, drips from the ceiling, and below it all a dull roar of a waterfall maybe. Perhaps it was the beast.

Two tentacles took hold of his legs. They pulled him through a darkened mist.

His body contracted and stretched by the tentacles.

Spots formed before his eyes. They morphed into hellish demons just beyond his field of vision. Jakub was enthralled by his imminent death. He laughed as reckless abandon overcame him. He felt as if he were a lad of eighteen, in his first battle.

Another tentacle grasped Jakub by the sword arm. It ripped his weapon away. Another tentacle squeezed Jakub around the waist. He felt his armor crack under pressure. Seconds expanded out into eternity. Could he give up? He could decide to die to be defeated by this beast what did it matter if his body was slowly digested. He had lost everything by becoming a vampire. All he had left was Agata.

Agata.

De Charney said a knight's lady could inspire great deeds in him. Jakub couldn't bare the thought of Agata weeping over his death.

He reached for the half-dead, but still screaming Timothé and caught his flailing arm. His fangs expanded. He ripped into gendarme's flesh. The man shrieked louder. His fear made his blood bitter, but Jakub needed his strength so Agata wouldn't weep. He wanted to feel the softness of her long black hair spilling across him once more.

He pulled a second blade from its scabbard and stabbed the tentacle which squeezed him. He did not want to die. He had promised his wife they would make a home in France together. It would be an eternity of love or at least of mutual respect

Jakub grunted in pain. Dazed, he swung his saber toward the fourth tentacle. Jakub felt the give of flesh. He shook his head to clear it as he scrambled to his feet.

He still hadn't found the entire beast. Only parts.

Grappling with the mounds of loose flopping flesh, Jakub shouted in fury. He had no idea how to find the vital organs.

He thought of a flea on a dog and bit into the flesh. Slime raced into open mouth and nose, burning, choking.

Jakub fought through thick mucus until his muscles cramped. He felt smothered. Then he tasted not mucous and slippery flesh but blood.

Blood.

He must find its heart.

With his blade, he dug deeper until he found a visceral

mass of organs coiled around one another. He cut through a sticky transparent membrane. Waste and offal spilled outward toward him.

He couldn't breathe. The stench was overwhelming.

He dug deeper and found its heart.

He bit into the two-chambered mass. Blood flowed into his mouth. He slurped it up until he believed he might drown.

He felt the same sense of loss after his father died, and his brother had inherited the county, but he was a grown man. And he had no tears for Gaius. Sitting in the darkness, he said, "I might have learned what Gaius could teach me." A strange thought overwhelmed him. He felt for the first time, he understood Gaius. The old general had created something in that old Carpathian fort. He had made peace with all the surrounding counts. For better or worse, Agata destroyed that peace. "That's why he hates her. That's why he came for me. He believes her malevolent."

He grunted as he pulled the beast by the tentacles. Slowly, inch by inch, he shifted it out of the cave, tearing its once majestic flesh. Once outside, using the swamp's slick mud, he was able to haul it on the cart. Seeing the cart without a driver, he remembered he had killed Timothé.

After preparing the horse, he hooked up Buttercup to cart. "I am more of a beast than the dreaded Lou Carcolh," he said to the mare. The sound of his voice felt deadened by the swamp. "And no one, but you, Buttercup, will ever know of my sin of eating Timothe. For this, you will be housed with honor in my own stables."

As he grew closer to civilization, a bitter, sour taste grew in his mouth. He wanted to celebrate his victory, yet it felt hollow. He had to kill a man to kill the monster.

✳

Chapter 23

AGATA'S EYES SPARKLED.

Would they sparkle if she knew what he had done? She rushed down the hall and threw herself in Jakub's filthy, slime-covered arms.

"My love, take care, don't spoil your fine gown," he said.

She threw her head back and laughed so hard that Jakub saw her fangs poking out of her gums in front of her other teeth. Her complexion grew ruddy and more alive. She had been feeding.

Jakub felt a lightness in his chest. He hoped she hadn't done anything ill-advised.

"Where is Gendarme deCaron?" she asked.

"The beast ate him."

"Sacrificed so you might defeat the Lou Carcolh?" she whispered.

Jakub stared at her for a moment.

How did she know? I guess Buttercup isn't the only one who would know.

Agata did not pull away from him. Her eyes sparkled though sadness faded their light. Still mesmerizingly vampiric. *Was she the evil entity that Gaius saw or was she my wife?*

"Fear not, a beauty such as Madame Caron won't be a widow for long." Agata said. "And her babies can still have a father. I am only sorry, because she did love him."

She pulled upon his arm and when he lowered his head to her, she whispered, "Your stepmother wishes for her own son to inherit his father's wealth. I had to protect you."

"Is the countess pregnant?"

"Of course not. She has an old man for a husband who has never fathered a child."

"Then why worry?"

"Because she has made it clear if the count realizes our true existence, we are in danger," Agata whispered.

"Danger?"

"If he realizes what we are, he might choose eternity rather than have a son. I dominated her to protect us with the promise you will take care of her in her dotage or see her married if she finds love."

"You, sweet wife, are wise beyond any woman or man, but now we are together again there is no need to fear anymore." Though he didn't feel like touching her lips, Jakub kissed her. He wanted to bathe.

His soon-to-be-father and stepmother exited the door, both were glaring at the scene. "And how did your adventure fare?" the countess asked softly.

"Countess." Jakub bowed. "I present to you, Lou Carcolh."

The countess left her husband's arm. She kissed Jakub on the cheek and then the other cheek. Then repeated the routine with Agata. "I am pleased to see our family finally grow. It seems to me, husband, that your son ought to have a statue raised in his honor."

Something was wrong. The woman he remembered would not speak so slowly. Was this what domination looked like on the outside?

"But Jakub did not defeat the task I asked him to accomplish," the count said. "Perhaps it is folly to make this man my son."

"You promised, husband," Countess Maria reminded

him.

Count Oliver didn't like to be reminded. He pinched his wife's arm. Her eyes screamed in pain, but she didn't whimper.

"Father, the Millet women, are not witches, just widows," Jakub said.

"In fact, when our own home is completed, I mean to invite the young Iuetta to work for us. The daughter is a bright hard-work girl, too young to live a life of solitude in the forest."

"Careful there, Lady Agata," Count Oliver warned. "The village still hates them. I would hate to see such a clever lady, especially one attached to my son, burned as a heretic because she made senseless decisions."

Agata lowered her eyes. "Did you know, Count Oliver, the inside of mussels create an expensive purple dye. I assisted your countess in the research."

"We wonder if this shell would also produce a specialty dye," Countess Maria said in the same slow, steady voice. "That might bring money back into the village, pay for the back taxes and secure Jakub's place as your son."

"What do women know of such things?" Count Oliver snapped.

"Lady Agata and I researched this problem," Countess Maria said though her voice wavered. "There was no folly in your son's slaying of this beast, rather than the Millet women."

"He is not my son, yet," Count Oliver replied.

Agata's eyes flashed to the countess. Jakub knew the other woman was not exactly under Agata's will. Indeed, it was as if the other woman was taking Agata's voice and inner strength. Yet, she was not a vampire. She was a human woman, outwardly frail.

"Husband, many are without employment," Countess Maria said. "We might use the giant shell to create our own unique pigment. With French court fashions, we might bring suitable trade here. Men who feed their families don't revolt.

"Just like in the days of old, the dyers keep the secret. The ancient Romans claimed the brew stunk, but since we have only one monstrous shell, we thought perhaps, dear husband, the townsfolk could create vats of dye and sell it slowly over an age to the crown."

"I shall think on it," Count Oliver said with a huff, but Jakub could see the old man's mind turning toward the suggestion.

"It is quite clever of my new mother to come up with such a plan," Jakub said.

"Yes, a godly woman can make the difference," the Count said, with marked bitterness in his voice. "As my wife cannot bring me a legitimate son, as promised, I will claim you as my legitimate son. Let us call the priest and the magistrate and be done with it."

Watching Count Oliver's retreating frame, Jakub knew he would lose his new father before long. He was an old man, hopefully he would die soon. Yet, if Death did not come, Agata would kill him for his ignoble actions.

Still it was hard to care about a man who accepted a noble's name and benefits, but not his responsibility to his vassals.

"Promise her, Jakub," Agata whispered.

De Charny gave a lady to leave her husband if he did not accomplish great deeds, but the Church did not. The King did not. Countess Maria was stuck in this corner of France without protection, no wonder she took Agata's strength.

Jakub kneeled. "I swear I will act as if you were my mother and you will be cared for as if I were your natural-born son. Better even.

"There is no need to fear any longer. A noble knight does not let a lady be harmed."

"Thank you, my son," she said in a more natural

voice, now that the count was gone. "Agata. You were right. I should not have doubted you."

*

March 1511

Chapter 24

JAKUB DID NOT WATCH THE MARBLE STATUE FORM in the town's square. It seemed uncouth somehow to expose oneself to one's own victories, especially when they had come at such a cost. He saw Timothé's face again and again in his mind.

The *Bible* offered him no comfort, nor did *Livre de chevalerie.*

He pretended to be human. He refused to eat the flesh of human persons and kept to the beef and lamb. Before dawn, he rose — even before the stable boy — to brush and bath his horse. As if he was a human, under heavy cloaks and a brimmed hat, he rode his horse through the village at dusk, took a night watch with the gendarmes, and rode again early in the morning.

During Lent, he fasted with the rest of the populace, which made his hunger more intense. He heard the villagers' heartbeats and dreamed how he wanted to rip into their bodies. Instead, he drank clear water. Jakub knew he was dangerous, more perilous than any wild animal in the forest to the populace. He was even more dangerous than Lou Carcolh, because he walked among them as a man in the image of God.

While meat was forbidden for Lent, every morning he sipped the blood which Agata brought him. As he knew the taste of their flesh, he learned to taste the differences in the blood of cows, lambs, goats, and pigs. He grew gaunt and his complexion became unhealthy.

He knew he didn't deserve the accolade, but by conquering the monster, his destiny became certain. Though he wished to leave it, he remained.

On the days approaching Easter festivities, one of the King's knights, Monsieur Michael De Paul, was welcomed into the manor. He was an older man whose scarred body and face showed his many battles. Jakub appreciated how he treated his squire, a boy of fifteen, and their horses.

When the sun rose on Saturday, Monsieur Michael went with Jakub to the family's chapel to make a confession. Since Jakub couldn't mention he was a vampire or even Oliver's adopted son, he simply said, "I feel unworthy. Timothé's sacrifice is the only way I was able to defeat the monster."

"All who battle feel guilty for surviving when their gendarme does not," the knight said.

Jakub wanted to cry out ifIhe hadn't killed Timothé for his blood, he wouldn't have the strength to kill Lou Carhol, but if he told these people that, he and his beloved would most likely be burned at the stake as sorcerers so he kept his mouth shut.

"Is there anything else?"

"I spoke with harshness to my valet," Jakub said.

Monsieur Michael and the priest seemed disappointed.

"Several times. I ought to be a better master," Jakub said. "The poor man has served my father before me, but I've been more short-tempered in my hunger during this Lent."

"Indeed, you should be a better master," the priest said.

"There is more, I think. You must be pure to be a knight," Monsieur Michael said with a knowing air that made Jakub think about ripping out his throat and tasting his warrior's blood.

"I've killed women and children."

"Battles are never clean, no matter what the populace wants to believe," Monsieur Michael said nodding.

"I lust after my wife, near constantly," Jakub said.

"God gave you a wife to bring forth children, not Earthly pleasures, contemplate upon this during your vigil," the priest said.

"Only your wife?" the knight said.

"My wife is both beautiful and clever. Only while at war, have I taken other women," Jakub said. "When I was a gendarme." He thought sadly, *I was not a gendarme, but a general of men, but that past is no more. Every moment, I become someone else, and even those who know don't care.*

"You must confess your sins." Monsieur Michael had been to war, he knew what soldiers did when away from their families, so though Jakub felt no shame, he confessed his infidelities. Since he could not confess his sins without harming his wife, he did not profess the iniquity which soaked his entire being. He could not tell the priest or knight that Agata was left alone to be raped by a vampire and murdered by a priest. If he had been there, he might have protected her. He had failed his lady.

Finally, the priest gave Jakub absolution.

Confession was followed by a long steaming bath. Jakub had to keep his body pure until he was knighted, but he wished Agata bathed him rather than Monsieur Michael. Once he was bathed and rested, the other knight dressed him in new white linens, followed by a finely woven red tunic, black hose, bound by a white belt of rope. Finally, he laid a scarlet cloak upon his shoulders.

Jakub returned to the chapel and kept vigil until the following morning. He did not pray, though many knights spent their vigil that way. Instead, he dreamed of the glory Gaius might find for different kings. And he thought of the demon horse, Nix. And decided it was a crime to give Castor the same fate. Castor deserved eternal rest in Paradise.

On Easter morning, church bells filled the air announcing the Resurrection of Christ.

The family filed into the chapel. The priest performed a mass for his new household. At the appropriate time, Jakub received Communion. The Host tasted like ash in his mouth, but Jakub swallowed it without fail. He half-hoped by the mounting doubt in his chest, the wafer would poison him. It did not.

Once the service ended, Monsieur Michael kissed Jakub's cheeks and bestowed upon him gilded spurs. He slapped his shoulders lightly with a double-edged sword, dubbing him "Monsieur Jakub," after which he presented the sword to him.

The sword's golden pummel and guard shined liked the sun. The fullered double-sided blade was lighter than his Moldavian sidearm. He felt a lump in his throat, he was not worthy to wield such a blade. Jakub had thought becoming a knight of the Empire of France might be the greatest moment of his existence, yet it felt like role-playing. He was not the son of Count Oliver. He wasn't even a human any longer.

However, he did not speak as he followed Monsieur Michael to the unveiling of his statue.

He watched the populace devouring eggs — a treat which had been forbidden during Lent — as they cheered. The thick tarp cracked and peerless, translucent, polished stone was uncovered.

His image held a sword over a massive cockle shell with swirling, twisting tendrils around him. His steely likeness was set in determination. Timothé's face was one of horror and pain; he tried to fight the beast's other spiraling tentacles.

The village cheered his name: "Monsieur Jakub." Instead of their voices, he only heard their thundering pulses. He wished he had felt worthy of such an honor, but the evil within his soul was just behind his eyes.

He only found gladness that the embossed copper plaque under the statue read: Monsieur Jakub de Banquier, son of Count Oliver, defeated Lou Carcolh by the sacrifice of his loyal and noble gendarme, Timothé deCaron.

"It is a great likeness," Agata said to the artist in French. "You have captured my handsome husband very well. Don't you think so, Countess Maria?"

The Countess murmured in agreement.

Jakub went to receive the honor from his new father and thank the young artist who created such a masterpiece. He had fought the battle to give Agata had a place in society. As long as their secret was kept, their problems were over, at least for now. But who knew what the centuries would bring? The thought of centuries without Castor brought tears to his eyes, but the thought of forcing Castor into eternity as a demon-horse, like poor Nix, made him weep.

Suddenly Monsieur Micheal had his arm. "Wipe your face, Monsieur. The cloak hides tears well enough," he whispered. Aloud to the crowd, Michael exclaimed: "It is good to weep for the fallen gendarme."

He did not know what was happening. Only that they were walking away from the crowds. Agata was on the other side of him.

"Don't fret so, my love," Agata whispered in Moldavian. "No doubt, God will send birds to shit on your statue."

Monsieur Michael must have understood at least part of Agata's words because he chuckled.

For a moment, Jakub was irritated, then he laughed.

"Your lady is clever. I feared you'd never crack a smile on this of all days," Monsieur Michael said.

"I take joy in the Resurrection, but the rest feels like theater," Jakub said to his mentor knight.

Monsieur Michael put his arm around Jakub's shoulders. "That ceremony is for the people. You and I know the battlefield. We know lies out there. By that look in her eyes, your lady has seen some sights that would make most ladies faint.

"The secret of your parentage is safe with me. I don't care, nor does the King, you are a bastard. That is why I am here and not some lesser man who was knighted after he was just a squire. Gods Blessings, Monsieur Jakub. See you at the feast."

"God's Blessings, Monsieur Michael."

And Jakub was alone with Agata again.

"Come," she said, "I've a shoulder of lamb for you. Lean on me if you need to, love."

Jakub felt guilty that his wife supported him. He ought to be strong enough to carry her across this village, but he wasn't. "How is it … "

"I never gave up meat this Lent," Agata said. "I feared I might not have your strength."

"You ate meat during Lent? You?" Jakub was becoming more annoyed at his wife.

"I gave up eating meat in God's likeness," Agata whispered. "Just animals."

He pushed her away from him. "I can make it on my own. Go back to the puppets," he hissed.

Confused by his rush of anger, he stormed to the manor's kitchens, where he found a shoulder of lamb waiting for him bubbling in its own juices and fat. He tore into the flesh without a word of thanks to the cook, not caring that he stained his knightly tunic.

As he ate, he remembered of Gaius's claim that immortality would kill their love. *Who knew what they would face in the coming centuries? What if Gaius had been right?*

*

June 1511

Chapter 25

AGATA DID NOT TRY TO HIDE HER JOY AND DELIGHT to see Irina's hand. Curious, yet fearing the news of her children, she scanned the letter quickly, knowing she could savor the sweet words again and again.

Dear Mamă and Tă, (Mama and Dad)

Congratulations, you are bunici!

The baby is a boy. He is a happy baby, and Lexi is quite a proud tă.

Since Lexi's tă is also an Alexander, as is his cousin, we didn't feel the need to name our firstborn after Lexi. Instead, we christened him Jakub.

Daciana is doing well. She has started reading the Proverbs aloud. Fortunately and unfortunately, she has taken some of it quite literally and will remind Petru of any minor misdeeds or mishaps.

She also knows all of the herbs and their uses. She does see Artur quite often and still follows him around. She rides her cousin's palfrey each day and speaks to it as you, Tă, speak to Castor. She has claimed she might become a sworn virgin so she might ride into battle with our brother. Whether this is a phase or her life only time will tell. For now, we appease her by asking her to practice herbery beside swordsmanship since if her fate is to become a soldier, then she ought to know healing for the good of her regiment.

Petru continues to do well under Lexi and Alexander. He has started to eye Fredrica Alexescue. He often sits with her family at church, and I saw them dancing at Easter. She is blossoming into a pretty girl and apprenticing to be an alewife. She has a good head on her shoulders, Mamă, and though she is a common girl, her family is reputable and kind. Neither her family or we have said much until we are sure this is not puppy love.

Artur has seen war, Tă, yet he remains as kind and gracious as ever. He has not forgiven himself for Mamă's injuries or that you and he parted in anger. He wishes for your blessing to marry Elena Julescue upon his eighteenth year. She is a fine girl, a year younger than he, from a family of furniture makers. Due to their craftsmanship and reputation, they have established themselves in the merchant class. Her family sent her to Aunt Gavrilla for finishing. Uncle has already blessed him, but he needs your blessings too and your forgiveness.

To answer your questions: we haven't seen any fish in the village, except when Uncle puts out the good bait on the seventh day after the full moon, but I will keep your recipes if they begin biting again.

The old trade agreements still stand for the good of all the Carpathian counties.

Please write again soon,

All my love,

Irina

Agata thanked God that it was overall good news. She wanted to find Jakub and share her pleasure, but her maid had questions and she was a lady of the French court now, the wife of a knight.

✱

JAKUB STARED AT THE FIRE AND FIDDLED WITH his elaborate oversized cuffs, which French fashion dictated were necessary. Since he became a knight, he had not slept, haunted by Gaius's words and de Charny's expectations. There had been no word from the King. With his new father's permission, he and Agata had moved into the old chateau and hired workmen to rebuild it. Once the dye trade had come, the old man became pliable toward his wife's suggestions. He saw her in a more favorable light which in turn made him see Agata more favorable as well. Thus he still lived.

Outside, masons slapped mortar onto bricks and stones, while workman hammered scaffolding. Further away, out in the workman's hut, he could hear bickering over a game. The workmen were paid and fed, but gambling and drinking would always be a problem.

Though this chamber had been cleaned and furnished, old dust filled his nostrils. Jakub ran his hand along the stone walls. The mortar between the stones was made of mud that held ancient blood spilled in battle. Jakub sensed the dead's presence. *Perhaps, war would come to France again.* One could only hope. *?* The only other two rooms that functioned were the corridor to the kitchen and the kitchen itself. It would be a decade at least until this house was restored. *Did our home in Moldavia feel so claustrophobic*

In the corridor, Agata's excited voice directed their two servants: a cook and a maid.

The maid — the older Millet girl, Iuletta, — asked a question about her duties. Her high-pitched question drilled into Jakub's brain, he imagined biting into her slender throat and drinking her dry. Outside, Agata answered with patience and kindness.

It is my duty to protect the commoners. I will not take my vassals' blood. I will not give my people any reason to doubt me. I need to know how to fight this senseless deterioration. Perhaps, my body no longer decays, but my mind and morals must return to the vows I once made for myself.

Why do I need war to endure?

Wishing for a true enemy, he obsessed about Gaius and wondered if the ancient vampire ever found his king. He speculated about the other vampires which he and Agata met on the road. None had been warriors, but that didn't mean none existed. If vampires attacked humans in his county, they must fall to his sword. He smiled at that thought. *Perhaps there are even other monsters that need culling.*

Agata came into the chamber, followed by her maid. Quiet as a mouse, Iuletta went to her seat in the corner to do some mending. He heard the girl's heartbeat and thought about the monster, which was hidden Jan inside his own body.

"My love, look! A letter from Irina! You must read it."

He looked up at his wife. Agata's gown could be of any French lady of the Court. Blackwork embroidered flowers that lined the edges of her square-necked chemise peeked out of her boldly patterned silk brocade. A gold lattice-work partlet was studded with pearls caught the light as she moved through the sitting room.

"What is wrong, my love?"

"This place seems empty and full at the same time," he said.

"Do you miss the children?" she asked.

"Of course," he answered, but he didn't know that was true that moment.

"I wished our children could have come with us to France," Agata said.

He glanced over her pearl covered shoulders and whispered in Moldavian, "Why do you believe in a God Who separated you from your children?"

Agata gestured something toward her maid. The girl curtsied and hurried out. "I believe in Him because the world is rich — far richer than we ever thought possible."

"And for this, these people would judge you as a heretic. So if this God came to you, right now?" Jakub asked.

"I would bow to Him, because no matter His other crimes, we exist together."

"And if I do not bow?"

"I would beg for your soul to remain beside mine," Agata said.

"The priests believe ... " Jakub trailed off.

Agata sat for a moment to ensure he was done before answering. "I do not care what men believe. They may be God's representatives, but they are not Gods. They are fallible."

Jakub was incensed by Agata's calm judgment. "My new father is right, my wife is a heretic."

"And you are an apostate, but I love you just the same," she said.

He was even more infuriated. He stormed out of the

small room, but remembered he had nowhere to go other than the kitchens. Outside, the sun was high. The maid trembled by the door but curtsied at him again. She kept her eyes to the floor. Around her neck, a silver chain sparkled. Agata had told him the girl knew of vampires.

"Bring my wife and I some wine," he growled at the girl. Bare feet slapping against the tile, she ran off toward the kitchens.

He turned back toward their only room.

"Do you wish to walk beside me for eternity?" Agata asked him in Moldavian. "I have a safe home again, a place in society. If you wish to go on knightly quests, I shall understand that a vassalage to protect is not the same as fighting for the honor of God."

"If He exists, I will not fight for His honor."

"The King then?"

"I don't know. When called, I must go."

"Do you still love me, Jakub?" Agata asked.

"Why ask that again? You are my wife."

"But do you love me?" Her voice trembled with terrible anguish.

"I long for a war to fight," He paused and collected his thoughts. "Gaius became a mercenary. I think he may be in Prussia. I see him in my dreams from time to time, but that is no life for a man with an honorable woman beside him."

She gently guided his chin and met his eye. "Do you wish to join him?"

"Yes," he said.

"Then, I set you free," Agata's voice cracked. She turned away, so he didn't see her eyes. "But before you go, read Irina's letter and answer it. Artur needs your blessing in marriage and you must forgive him for what happened."

"I don't blame the boy."

"Then you must tell him that — in your own hand."

He looked at his sword, hanging on the weapons

rack. There was a moment that he felt free of the eternal responsibility of a wife. A sudden manifestation of the essential nature of reality ripped through his heart. Gaius could teach him to be a warrior vampire, but there would be no love or chivalry or any other tenet which he had built his life upon in that existence. He had killed countless people on the battlefield, it was not magnificent. It had only been one bloody mess after another.

If he truly believed in chivalry, his new battle was how to remain a knight while being a vampire. He needed to confess the sin on his heart which slowly picked away at their love. Not to the priests. They did not matter.

"I don't blame our son or you," he said, "I blame myself for what happened to you."

"You weren't there," Agata said. There was no rebuke. There never was.

"I should have been. There was always a war to fight, a prince to serve. That meant I left my lady alone, which is why I shall not leave now.

"If the King calls, I must ride or send someone in my stead, but I doubt he will. At least not this King, perhaps the next will call for Jakub's son, Jakub. For now I must remain here and protect this county," Jakub said. "There is no path to glory except by conquering the monster inside me. I confront it each time a living heart moves near me."

"Then why pine for what you cannot have?" she asked, her soft lips quivering.

"For the same reason, you pine for the children." He wrapped his arms around Agata. He kissed her brow, each of her cheeks, and lips. "I miss our previous existence. I might grieve, but I would not be one of the vampires wandering the countryside in rags. And I'd not have you be one either. Or Castor.

"I conquered Lou Carcolh so our love would have a place in this world, but I was only able to do that by killing.

To survive as vampires, I must grow to become a man of peace and protect those in my vassalage. Kings, the Church, none of that matters. We will watch all of it rise and fall and rise again."

Jakub kneeled in front of his wife and clasped her hands in his. "Eternity will be long, but love is rare and precious, and I swear to protect our love above all else."

Agata bestowed kisses upon him. Unlike his public accolade, this one was mattered.

The End

ABOUT THE AUTHOR

Elizabeth Guizzetti lives in Seattle with her husband. When not writing or illustrating, she loves hiking and birdwatching. She also enjoys to watch professional wrestling. To find out more about her work follow her on Twitter @E_Guizzetti or Instagram @e_guizzetti or Facebook /Elizabeth.Guizzetti.Author

Other Works

Paper Flower Consortium Universe Books
Accident Among Vampires
Honor Among Vampires
Immortal House: A Nightmarish Tale of Vampires and Real Estate
Norma's Cleaning Service Mysteries
Death Pulls a Stake Out
Death Hears a Siren
Death Sticks a Pixie
Podcasts
The Paper Flower Consortium

Novels and Novellas
Other Systems
The Light Side of the Moon
The Grove

Chronicles of the Martlet
The War Ender's Apprentice: Book 1
The Morality of a Necromancer: Book 2
The Assassin's Twisted Path: Book 3

Comics and Illustration Projects

Faminelands
Out For Souls & Cookies!
Lure
For the Love of Pancakes
A is for Apex written by Jennifer Brozek
The Prince of Artemis V written by Jennifer Brozek